Henry King Lewis

The Child

its spiritual nature

Henry King Lewis

The Child
its spiritual nature

ISBN/EAN: 9783337332693

Printed in Europe, USA, Canada, Australia, Japan

Cover: Foto ©Andreas Hilbeck / pixelio.de

More available books at **www.hansebooks.com**

THE CHILD

ITS SPIRITUAL NATURE

BY

HENRY KING LEWIS

COMPILER OF "SONGS FOR LITTLE SINGERS IN THE SUNDAY SCHOOL AND HOME"

London
MACMILLAN & CO., Ltd.
New York
THE MACMILLAN CO.
1896

"If religion cannot accommodate itself on the one side to the capacity of children, or if on the other side it fails to satisfy the requirements of men, it has lost its vitality, and it becomes mere superstition or mere philosophy."—MAX MÜLLER.

PREFACE.

It is unnecessary to say more here than that the tracing of the mental and physical aspects of childhood, intensely interesting and highly important as they are, must be regarded as quite subordinate to the point of view from which the child is contemplated in these pages, namely, the Spiritual. The mental, as well as the corporeal, are now receiving deserved investigation, but the Spiritual has been almost exclusively in the hands of those whose special purpose has been the classification of the various qualities of spirit according to the theological system whose claims they accept, usually as a theoretical assumption.

But the question is not one of theory or theology only, but is of intense practical importance, for as is the child so will the man become.

A few illustrations have been introduced of typical children, and of some of these stories are given under their respective headings in the following pages.

Grateful acknowledgments are due to many parents who have kindly assisted the author with trustworthy facts from their own family records, besides which many illustrative instances are selected from historical sources which are generally available.

H. K. L.

June, 1896.

CONTENTS.

FRONTISPIECE.

These three children of one family express a common hereditariness, and a striking evolution of mental capacity, in the power of appreciation of the photographic process through which they are passing. The youngest is excited, the next is characterised by a quiet appreciation, and the eldest is more quiescent and satisfied.

Some stories of the children depicted in the frontispiece are incorporated in the text of the book. The illustration is introduced specially for the representation by the three children of the phases of mind and character in the same family, and the growth of the faculties of body, soul and spirit, which are gradually unfolding in expressiveness and power.

By the kind permission of Mr. Arthur Reston, Photographic Artist, Stretford, near Manchester.

THE CHILD

ESPECIALLY CONSIDERED WITH REFERENCE TO ITS

SPIRITUAL NATURE AND POSSIBILITIES.

———•———

CHAPTER I.

INTRODUCTION

OF all the promising and only partially-developed fields of human enquiry, none is more remarkable than that of Childhood. Till within a comparatively recent date, but little had been done by science in the investigation of the subject. Physiology and medicine took cognisance of childhood mainly for the light their researches might throw on the adult and his ailments. The modern humane and rational treatment of mental disorders gave a great impetus to the study of Psychology, a study in which childhood has come in for a considerable share.

To the philosophers of ancient Greece and Rome a child, for its own sake, was of no particular value as a subject of serious inquiry. Yet what the embryo is to the new-born babe, that essentially is the infant child to the full-grown man. The axioms of heathen

philosophy were derived from far too narrow an induction, and human wisdom never dreamt of putting
a little child in the midst of the ancient sages.

With uncultured peoples children became a species
of property, and would be dealt with according to the
kind and degree of civilization to which they had
attained.

In comparison with the life and history of surrounding nationalities, Judaism sustains a position of marked
superiority—a fact which may surely be regarded as a
demonstration of the Being and attributes of God.
For He, through Moses, was the Teacher and Law-
giver of Israel.

In the claims of parental authority, and in the reverence enjoined on their children, the legislation of Israel
set up an ideal of which other civilizations gave
scarcely a hint. The domestic affections were fostered; and from Abraham onwards, we see how life
shaped itself, in the interests of the children and especially the sons. Discipline was maintained by very
severe enactments, such as capital punishment for the
striker or reviler of a parent, though not at the independent will or caprice of that relative.

But when we come to the study of the life of Jesus
Christ, we have reached a new departure. The claims
of the woman, the mother, as well as the child, receive
recognition, and to them is assigned a position they
never before occupied; and the primary object
throughout this book is to follow the great Teacher

in His estimate of a little child; to trace its spiritual possibilities in the light of His doctrine, and to encourage the preparation of the ground for that higher training of children, which a true appreciation of the subject demands.

It is proposed, then, first, to discuss the child in his essential attributes, mental, moral, and spiritual; and the physical only as it stands in subordinate relation to, or affects the higher faculties of the child's nature. Perez, Sully, Ferrier, Herbert Spencer, Houzeau and others, have supplied minute and most valuable information on the early stages of childhood and make it unnecessary to go over ground they have so well occupied.

As education, both in its principles and methods, has assumed the character of a modern science, so the study of the creature to be educated or developed grows more intensely interesting. Educational practice will be brought more closely into harmony with the accepted principles, as the requirements of the nature to be developed are recognized.

We want to handle the child, as we find him, with his ascertainable limitations, and his actual possibilities. For the discovery of these limits and possibilities can we adopt a more satisfactory course than that which the inductive method supplies?

We must protest, most vigorously, against beginning with theory, whether philosophical or theological. Living, healthy specimens are always to be had, until tampered with by quacks. The most promising samples, therefore, if the most reliable results are to be secured, will be those that are taken from the earliest moment possible.

Let these be studied, analysed, compared and classi-fied. A fairly sound generalization will then be pos-sible.

He who would obtain satisfactory results, must come to the consideration of the subject with an open mind, free from any foregone conclusions. We do not seek an acquaintance with Egyptian life and character within the folds of a mummy cloth, nor is the attempt to ascertain and describe the qualities of a living child of to-day likely to be a successful one, if we conduct our investigations on a child full of hereditary taints, any more than among the dry specimens in some old theological museum.

We shall first put aside all *à priori* theories, and proceed at once to trace, in the dawn of intelligence, perception, emotion, volition, &c, those attributes with which this marvellous little creature—a child—is en-dowed.

We shall then consider some of the more general conditions under which the child's character is modi-fied, though in its essential attributes it must remain unaltered. These conditions will include the question of evolution, heredity, nationality, climate, and not least, religion.

The influence of a child on parent and the family

generally, in the development of human affection, self-denial, and refinement of manners, may be briefly discussed in a supplementary section.

But where there is no light, the habitations of cruelty reveal the hardness of heart, which leads to the brutal sacrifice of children, or their gross ill-treatment. Thanks to the Rev. Benjamin Waugh, for his valuable and successful efforts in our own country, to expose and correct this crying evil.

The ultimate purpose of the book is Christian life. In Christ, the boy, we have the ideal child; and in His teaching we are furnished with the laws of a Kingdom which is based upon true childhood. His words contain enough, and more than enough, to correct the misconceptions which for ages have tended to obscure or pervert the "simplicity that is in Christ."

CHAPTER II.

THE HUMAN MIND IN INFANCY AND CHILDHOOD.

THE new-born babe is the most helpless creature that comes into the world. Hence it is that, to the earnest inquirer, its earliest years are watched with the most fruitful results. Of all the arts of restraint, or disguise, or exaggeration or simulation, to the practice of which the temptation is so strong in later years, the infant is in guileless and blissful ignorance. You approach the child as a discoverer, and if your specimen be a poor one, be sure it is due to no fault of the child. The child offers no discouragement to the fullest inquiry.

Nevertheless the child is not idle. Its receptive faculties begin to open with its earliest breath; and though at first all movements must be automatic, it is wonderful how soon a motive for action may be discovered. It strikes out right and left, with all its four limbs. It is stimulated to give expression to its feelings, by the contact of the surrounding air with its breathing apparatus; and its inarticulate cries awaken the solicitude of the mother. Nutriment and repose on the mother's breast are at hand.

As a rule, visual perception of objects takes place after three or four weeks. Tiedemann recorded the

This picture shows the same boy at various ages.

The baby reveals the active nature of the child in the exercise of the prehensile powers over the feet, while there is as yet scarcely anything more than automatic action. There is an intermediate stage in the left side picture of the child which impresses with its intelligence, and strongly foretells the coming man. In the central figure the boy has developed physically in active energy and strength, and makes good promise of being at the top of his class, and foremost at boating or cricket.

almost incredible observation that movements of the eyes have been observed the second day after birth. The action could be simply reflex, due to the vibration of light. But just as we are struck with admiration at the first successful experiment in the use of a delicately-constructed bit of mechanism, so do those who watch the complex organization of a newly-born babe mark with delight and satisfaction the evidences of healthy function.

The slow progress of development in a child, in comparison with other animals, is illustrated in the fact that in a month a kitten will make as much progress in physical development as a child accomplishes in two years.

An infant is susceptible of great enjoyment. Fresh surprises are continually opening up with its expanding powers: and it is remarkable how many and how varied are its pleasures, acquired through sight and hearing and touch, with a rapidly increasing capacity through their use.

The study of the phenomena of mind in childhood is very interesting to parents; and love and thoughtfulness often record the original remarks of their children from year to year.

These observations are most valuable, as affording illustrations of the discrimination of facts, the mode of reasoning, and the conclusions—often strange and unexpected—at which the infant arrives.

As supplying the psychologist with the means of

appreciating the character and state of mental progress of the child, these recorded phenomena are
exceedingly useful. Not less important are they as
disclosing the data of moral consciousness, and their
influence in the formation of character.

Comparison of one period with another in the progress of a child's life, furnishes the opportunity for
tracing the growth of the child's mind, a practice
which parents have sometimes wisely adopted.

Before we pass on to some more special considerations, we may observe how facts to be adduced tend
to illustrate or to oppose certain general conclusions
current among us as to child-nature.

Of all the phenomena of nature, in the heavens or
on the earth, that call forth our wonder and admiration, that stimulate our interest and warm our affections, or that awaken our anticipations for the future,
or that afford scope for the imagination, nothing is
comparable to the little child.

Perhaps Wordsworth is unsurpassed as the poet of
childhood, when he sings :—

> Our birth is but a sleep and a forgetting;
> The Soul that rises with us, our life's Star,
> Hath had elsewhere its setting,
> And cometh from afar:
> Not in entire forgetfulness,
> And not in utter nakedness,
> But trailing clouds of glory do we come
> From God, who is our home;

Heaven lies about us in our infancy,
Shades of the prison house begin to close
    Upon the growing Boy,
But he beholds the light, and whence it flows,
    He sees it in his joy.
The Youth, who daily farther from the east
    Must travel, still is Nature's priest,
    And by the vision splendid
    Is on his way attended ;
At length the Man perceives it die away
And fade into the light of common day.

Nor have the poets failed to perceive wherein the strength of a little child is found. In the babe we have before our eyes continually a form of omnipotence. The infant's strength is its weakness—" the weakness of God is stronger than men."

This is prettily embodied in some verses by John Dennis :—

THE MASTER OF THE HOUSE.

He cannot walk, he cannot speak,
    Nothing he knows of books and men,
He is the weakest of the weak,
    And has not strength to hold a pen ;
He has no pocket, and no purse,
    Nor ever yet has owned a penny,
But has more riches than his nurse,
    Because he wants not any.

He rules his parents by a cry,
    And holds them captive by a smile,
A despot, strong through infancy,
    A king, from lack of guile.

He lies upon his back and crows,
  Or looks with grave eyes on his mother,
What can he mean ? But I suppose
  They understand each other.

Indoors or out, early or late,
  There is no limit to his sway,
For wrapped in baby robes of state,
  He governs night and day.
Kisses he takes as rightful due,
  And, Turk-like, has his slaves to dress him.
His subjects bend before him too,
  I'm one of them.   God bless him !

The following observations and original facts, some-what roughly classified, include the sayings of small children, and the childhood of persons who became remarkable ; together with some of the conclusions arrived at by careful and earnest investigators.

Many of these facts especially afford illustrations of the qualities and tendencies of the child, as a spiritual being.

They are selected primarily as foreshadowing the mature individual as he would be, unbiassed by undue social influences, wise or otherwise, and untrammeled by the artificialities of modern education.

Ineffaceableness of early impressions.

The earliest impressions on the mind of a child, whether sensuous, mental, or spiritual, are very deep, and not seldom ineffaceable. As a striking illustration of the fact we take the following summary gathered from Hodder's " Life of the Earl of Shaftesbury," and having read the account, let the reader look at a good portrait of the late Earl and he will see the early life quite vividly depicted in his expressive face.

" Although not yet seven years of age, there was in his heart a distinct yearning for God." Maria Miller had been his mother's nurse, and she was now house-keeper. She formed a strong attachment for the gentle, serious child, and would take him on her knee and tell him Bible stories, especially the sweet stories of the Manger, of Bethlehem, and the Cross of Calvary. *It was her hand that touched the chords* and awakened the first music of his spiritual life. At the age of seven, young Ashley went to school—Manor House School, Chiswick—*now* an Asylum for the Insane. It was a dreadful school ; it might almost be called a school for making insane boys. " The young days of his life, instead of being full of brightness, and sunshine, and merriment, were made utterly wretched. Even in old age he would say :—' The memory of that place makes me shudder ; it is repulsive to me even now. I think there never was such a wicked school before or since. The place was bad, wicked, filthy ; and the treatment was starvation and cruelty.' . . . . . ." He clung to his old friend, for she was the only grown-up person in the world he really loved ; the only one to whom he had dared to speak of the misery of his school life, the only one with whom bright and beautiful memories of his earlier years were associated. In her will she left him her gold watch, and until the day of his death, he never wore any other. He was fond even to the last of showing it, and would say, "that was given to me by the best friend I ever had in the world."

That early impressions are deep, has been accounted for, at least in part, by Mrs. Child, Mass., U.S., who says :—" The mind of a child is not like that of a grown-up person, too full and too wordy to observe anything. It is a vessel always ready to receive and always receiving," or it is like "wax to receive and marble to retain."

Intuitive Discrimination of Character.

Children are not slow in the detection of character. Their sympathies are as readily drawn out to some, as their antipathies are aroused towards others. As in the vegetable world a young and sensitive plant yields itself to the tender and silent attraction of the sunshine, so will a responsively loving heart of a child be drawn out even before a word has been spoken, or the critical faculty has had a chance of asserting its authority; and, as a rule, the intuitive response to a kindly attractive face or touch will be a truthful one.

James Hogg, the Ettrick shepherd, says :—" It is a curious fact that children are the best judges of character at first sight in the world. There is an old Scotch proverb, 'they are never cannie, that dogs' and bairns dinna like' and there is not a more true one in the whole collection."

Assuming the spirituality of child-nature, ought we to be in the least surprised at such an indication as this?

"The spirit of man that is in him," precedes intellectual processes in the development of mind. Childhood has been misunderstood, mainly because its spirituality has been ignored. St. Paul's profound proposition that "he that is spiritual discerneth all things, while he himself is discerned of no man" (I. Cor. ii. 15), finds striking illustrations in many a child's observations.

Percy (nine years old) hopes he shall grow up like papa, both in face and character; he thinks his father as near perfection as possible. (And those who know papa, admire Percy's discrimination).

A little child lives by faith, before the perceptive faculties of the mind are awakened to anything in the shape of a creed in its most elementary form. Of this fact we have a remarkable illustration in the personal recollections of George Sand.

"I walked at ten months. I talked pretty late, but when once I had begun to say a few words, I learnt all the words very quickly, and at four I could read very well. I was also taught prayers; I remember that I said them, without stumbling, from beginning to end, and without understanding a syllable, except these words when I and my cousin Clotilde, were laying our heads on the same pillow, 'My God, I give you my heart.' I don't know why I understood that more than the rest, for there is much that is metaphysical in these two words; however I *did* understand them, and it was the only part of my prayers in which I had some idea of God, and of myself. As to the Pater, the Credo, and the Ave Maria which I knew very well in French, except 'Give us this day our daily bread,' I might just as well have said them in Latin like a parrot, they would not have been more unintelligible to me."

The Essential and the Accidental.

It is necessary to distinguish between what is *essential*, and what is *accidental* in this as in every other subject proposed for our consideration. A jewel in the diadem of a queen is essentially the same as a jewel on a dungheap.

In his diary, Lord Shaftesbury writes :—" At Manchester, I perambulated the town on Saturday night in company with two inspectors, and passed through cellars, garrets, gin-palaces, beer-houses, brothels, gaming-houses, and every resort of vice and violence. . . . . . . Saw *a darling little girl*, seven years old, in the very depth of dirt and uproar. Never did I witness such beauty of natural, untaught affection towards its rough and unkind mother."

Freedom.

The love of liberty is early manifested in a babe, and one of the first things to which it awakes is a sense of restraint. The struggle for freedom is perhaps the earliest effort it puts forth. "The heart may be a free and fetterless thing," but the heart is quickly engaged in conflict with its environment.

It comes into the world under a system of Law, and more often than not, it learns obedience through the things it suffers, especially at the hands of stupid and ignorant mothers and nurses. Coming from the land of liberty—Heaven itself—it soon discovers that it is cabined, cribbed, confined.

Clothes.

Children are often compelled to think of their clothes as of greater importance than *themselves.*

Admiration for the dress is often sought by a fond mother ; or of a pretty child, for its face, as though either were of primary importance. Children catch the idea, and learn to measure themselves and others by this merely outward standard.

"Happy he who can look through the Clothes of a Man (the woollen, and fleshly, and official Bank-paper and State-paper Clothes), into the Man himself ; and

discern, it may be, in this or the other Dread Poten-
tate, a more or less incompetent Digestive-apparatus;
yet also an inscrutable venerable Mystery, in the
meanest Tinker that sees with eyes!"*

There is that in clothes which little children are
decidedly opposed to. Clothes with their bands and
buttons are a restraint. They rejoice to get out of
them and to feel unfettered. The mother strips the
child for bed. Escaped from its last garment, the little
elf dashes off, dances, runs round the room, exulting in
a sense of freedom in God's air.

The soul has been sometimes put into old folks'
clothes. How ludicrous they are felt to be! Calvin-
istic buckram that chafes the skin; small clothes that
are much too small for the little soul. Can the souls
of grown up men and women be really smaller than the
souls of their babes? Yea, quite possible.

Cloaks.

A cloak seems to be more tolerable to a little child
than clothes, it does not so largely deprive it of its
sense of freedom. But when, by wrong-doing, it has
ceased to be a little child, its spiritual nature is hurt,
and it seeks to conceal the self-inflicted wound by any
fig-leaf it can lay its hands on.

* Carlyle's *Sartor Resartus.*

Heaven.

We cannot help associating an infant with heaven. If we accept the Christ, we must believe the connection is a very real one.

Heaven is a revelation of God. God makes Heaven. It is a thought of His mind; it is an unfolding of His love. It is an expression of His will. Our loved ones gather there, and in joining the heavenly throng the divine idea acquires wider expansion, the divine pulse throbs through the ever-growing body, and the divine will attains deeper and fuller significance.

But God has revealed Himself in our sunny skies, our rolling seas, and our flower-adorned earth ; in all the wonderful changes and developments of nature— in human life—with its joys and sorrows—its splendid careers and heroisms !

And the most beautiful aspect of the revelation of God comes to us in childhood, untouched by temptation, untarnished by sin. The revelation of God in Heaven may never be clouded by imperfect vision, or obscured by sin ; on earth it is different, but the manifestation is the same for all that.

If the world of humanity in its origin and destiny is not of God whence can it be ? " The Earth is the Lord's, and the fulness thereof."

" The (to us) unknown future world is but a manifestation of God Almighty's will, and a development of nature neither more nor less than this in which we are, and an angel glorified or a sparrow on a gutter, are equally parts of His Creation."*

Yet the conception of heaven as brought before the mind of a little child, is commonly so materialistic, and the occupations of the redeemed so utterly beyond anything a child can make out, that an honest, healthy boy can hardly be got to express a willingness, much less a longing to go.   And should he?

But here is the candid utterance of a little boy whose notion of heaven was acquired in a well-known school. Tom's aspirations are rather languid; he thinks heaven must be a dull place.   His conclusion that it must be so, is based on the observations he has made at church. Faces solemn, and often sad; surely heaven must be worse than school.   With heaven on the brain, he said one day to his mother:—" Mother, I hope when I go to heaven, they will let me have a Saturday half-holiday that I may go and have a game in hell."

Pity.

Pity—"akin to love "—this is a profound spiritual affection, whose root is sympathy. "Thine eye pitied."

How readily it is evoked towards those who have the care of children.   The nurse-girl's "Ah, poor!" and the tender feeling aroused towards herself; or it

* Thackeray's *Letters.*

may be, as she strokes the fur of the cat, the same feeling is called forth from a very little child indeed.

How opposed to *cruelty* is this divine virtue. St. Paul uses the phrase " bowels of compassion," expressive of this divine element of pity.

Many of our affections bring with their exercise unmitigated pleasure; but pity for the sufferings or misfortunes of others evokes a sympathy whose tenderness is sad if not positively distressing. Hence there can be no self-seeking here. It is not a seeking of self-gratification (which the exercise of a feeling of benevolence may be) and therefore must rank very high as a divine faculty of the soul. We know how distressed a little child may be when the function of pity is excited.

Mabel (four) in the garden would call, "Come, pretty birds, we won't hurt you. Do come." Catching a butterfly, she was so grieved at the injury inflicted on the fragile thing, that she determined that she would never try to catch another.

One day Muriel, when three years of age, was found kneeling on her bed looking intently at a picture of our Lord's Crucifixion, and when asked by her mother what she was doing, replied with tears in her eyes, "Oh mother, why don't they take out the nails?"

The blissful ignorance of little children.

" Bacon openly taught, as a fundamental principle of his method, that men must enter the Kingdom of

Science, as Christ taught His disciples to enter the Kingdom of Heaven, by becoming as little children."*

"But it was impossible that Science should make any progress, while every fact of every-day life, almost, was explained by false theories and erroneous assumptions. All these things had to be *ignored*. Just so, also, the true knowledge of God and Jesus Christ was rendered almost impossible, through the traditions and theological assumptions of priests and teachers. All this had to be ignored."†

Little children are happily *ignorant*, and when light shines on them, they find it pleasant, and in the light they can walk. *Knowing nothing at all* is the very best condition for revelations from the Father. "I determined to know nothing," &c., says St. Paul; and he would have his converts "wise concerning that which is good and simple (ignorant) concerning that which is evil."

Contentment.

Bacon, in his *Advancement of Learning*, says :—" In divine truth a man cannot endure to become a little child "; but a healthy child feels it no degradation to be a child. It is content with its natural condition.

At first, a child cannot endure to be made what he is not ; but he soon *learns* to give himself airs, and alas ! he is no longer a little child.

* Strutt's *Inductive Method*, p. 5.
† *Ibid*, p. 6.

Orderliness.

Order, as distinguished from confusion, is hardly to be expected in a child. Discrimination of the ever-increasing number and variety of its facts, their relative importance, and the multiplicity of things a child can handle, are not likely at a very early date to fall under any orderly arrangement.

But here is an instance of an orderly mind:—Edith (before two) would have all the doll's clothes folded and put away exactly in their right places.

A still more remarkable example we have in the boyhood of Mr. Gladstone, whose daughter, Mrs. Drew, mentions that his first well-authenticated words were:—" Take it away; how can I do two things at once?" He was then a small boy doing his lessons, when he was interrupted by the entrance of the nurse bringing him a dose of physic. "The words," remarks Mrs. Drew, " will seem to some foreshadowing of the astuteness of the old parliamentary hand who finds an escape out of any situation, but to those who know Mr. Gladstone more than superficially they contain one of the secrets of the assurance of his convictions and the success of his work."

As boys, Cavendish and Sir Humphrey Davy were remarkable contrasts. The former was retiring in disposition, and studious; escaping from society where he might be brilliant. The latter would fancy himself a lecturer, before a vast gathering of eager listeners, and would carefully arrange his imaginary auditorium.

Before we leave the more spiritual aspects of the child-nature, to discuss the development of the intellectual faculties, many instances of the practical indications of religious principles may be adduced.

Prayer and practice—faith and works.

Dr. Hamilton, of Regent Square Church, in his interesting *Memories*, relates a prayer uttered by one of his infant children. " O Lord, open pussy's eyes, and make her tail grow "—a prayer which in due time was answered.

It would indeed be strange if in a little child no trace could be discovered of his origin as the offspring of the great Father in Heaven. We are not surprised at such a story as this, related by Mrs. Cadby, of a child's faith in God.

Children at a very early age are able to appreciate God's loving care and protection, and their pure, unsullied trust has often helped the waning faith of their elders. This was seen in the case of a little boy eight years of age who had just lost his father after a lingering illness. The mother in her heart-breaking grief and desolation said to the child :—" Oh ! my boy, we are *alone now*." But the boy's faith was unshaken, and he replied with an emphasis which astonished and almost reproved the mother:—" No, Mamma, we are *not alone,* for *God is with us!*"

A little girl told a friend who was visiting her father that her brothers set traps to catch the birds. He asked her what she did. She replied, " I prayed that the traps might not catch the birds." " Anything else ? " " Yes," she said, " I then prayed that God would prevent the birds getting into the traps ; " and, as if to illustrate the doctrine of faith and works, she added, " I went and kicked the traps all to pieces."

" The most perfect prayers are those of Saints and of little children, because in both there is the same freedom from the hard, unconcerned, self-contemplative habit of mind which besets the common sort of Christians, and the same presence of awe, tenderness of conscience, simplicity and truth."—*Cardinal Manning.*

When he was only four years old Father Damien was missed from home, and was found alone in the church of a neighbouring village where a fair was going on, praying under the pulpit.

Godliness.

Harold (seven) speaking of what he would choose to be when a man, said " I don't mean to choose anything, I am going to do what God pleases."

Holiness.

" The holiness of children is the very type of saintliness ; and the most perfect conversion is but a hard
and distant return to the holiness of a child."—*Cardinal
Manning.*

Atonement and reconciliation.

A packet of sweets was given to a child, and his
mother wisely took charge of it, since the child did not
and could not know that to eat them all at one time
would be injurious. Unfortunately the packet was
left on a shelf within reach of the little one, and he
knew it. Two hours afterwards—a long interval for
a child who has set his heart upon a sweet—the little
boy was heard calling for his mother or anybody who
would give him a sweet, one of *his own* sweets. Everybody was busy and no one could listen to the poor
little fellow. He got upon a chair and reached the
packet of sweets, and then went about the house seeking someone to give him permission to gratify his
longing. Nobody was within call. What was he to
do ? They belonged to him ; he had not had one, and
he took one. It was an act of disobedience and he
knew it. When his father saw him a few minutes
later, he had popped the tempting candy into his
mouth. The little fellow had now realised the terrors
of broken law. His heart was quickly broken. He

went about the house crying piteously. He came to his grandmother. She tried to comfort him. He told her without hesitation of his offence. She endeavoured to divert his mind to something else, a very wise and proper thing to do had it been a case of physical suffering; but he would not be comforted. His heart was broken; there was a temporary break in the sacred relationship of child and parent. Was it right to attempt to stop the crying by diverting his attention from the more serious spiritual hurt? No, the child felt that it would not do. He must be healed, and he could not be healed by *looking the other way.* The child was truer to his nature than was the grandmother. In his heart he was saying " I want atonement; I must be reconciled." He slipped off his grandmother's knee, he could not wait; he sought and found his parents. The reconciliation was effected. The equilibrium of his moral life was restored. The tears were wiped away. The smile of peace soon flitted across his countenance and his strength was renewed. He took no more sweets. They ought not to have been left within his reach. " Lead us: not into temptation, but deliver us from evil." But how intensely spiritual was this moral evolution!

Restraint and liberty.

You walk with a child of three or four years. You take its hand, to ensure its keeping your pace. The child drags behind. You feel that he wants to break away; to take his own steps, so different from *yours*—yours, proper to you, but not to the child. He struggles to be free, and at length you relax your grasp of his hand. He is free; he drags no more now; there is no hanging back; he rejoices in his freedom, and he shows it by trotting along quite ahead of you, and you have to quicken your pace to keep up with him.

Are there not often enforced on little children restraints as foolish as they are unnatural? Keep the child on the lines of nature, for these are the ways of grace. " Then shall I run in the ways of Thy commandments when I am enlarged," *i.e.*, set at liberty.

Intelligent appreciation and sympathy are suggested by the divine promise, " I will guide thee with mine eye "—not by force, but by loving sympathetic *wisdom*.

The shadow of a father's guilt on an innocent child.

William Whittam—one of a gang of burglars—wrote a long letter to his wife, detailing several attempts he had made to escape from prison. The letter was intercepted by the jailor. It was of considerable length, and well expressed. It contained the following :—"... Kiss dear little Nellie. I can't get her out of my thoughts. *She seems to know there is something wrong, the funny way she looks at me.*"

The scape-goat !

A STORY OF SIR EDWARD BURNE-JONES.—Sir, then Mr., Burne-Jones had so far recovered from the effects of a recent fall that he was able to paint for several hours during the period of his convalescence. One of the earliest exercises of his art after his recovery was characteristic. Being at the house of a friend, he found himself in the nursery, and there the child-daughter of the house was for some nursery offence undergoing solitary confinement in a corner. When the authorities came to release the tiny prisoner they found the walls of her cell covered with beautiful pencil drawings of flights of birds, and all sorts of scenes of "faery lands forlorn." Half frightened and half proud, the little one explained, quite unnecessarily :—" Please, it wasn't I ; 'twas Mr. Burne-Jones that did it."

A boy's self-sacrifice.

" An orphan boy and his hungry mongrel dog were the objects of universal dislike and ridicule in the house of his uncle, a Scotch farmer. The lad always sat of an evening far back from the circle of the fire-side, with his crouching dog under his stool lest it should be kicked. One day the little son of the house, of whom the farmer and his wife were dotingly fond, went out with the boy and dog, and a snow-storm

coming on they were all lost on the hills. Next morning the dog returned to the farm, making wild signs
that the farmer should follow him, which he and his
wife did at once, in great anxiety. At last the dog
brought them to a spot where they found the boy stiff
and cold, but their own child still alive. The boy had
taken off his own coat and wrapped it round the child,
whom he laid on his breast, and then, lying under him
on the snow, he died."*

Another illustration of self-sacrifice. It is Christmas weather, and if you pull aside the curtains and
look out into the street you can see two little boys,
just outside the window. The younger one is sitting
upright in the hand-cart, and his big brother—who
must almost be able to write his age with two figures—
is pushing him along. Is it a colder blast than usual,
or why do they pull up for a talk together? You
notice them, with their patched and darned clothes,
and then, as you watch, you see the elder take off his
poor little coat, and in the tenderest way begin to
wrap it round his little brother. He is in his shirt
now, and the wind blowing through the thin ragged
cotton, but he does not seem to care—one at any rate
shall be warm. And sure that his little brother is now
well protected, he stoops over and gives him a kiss;
aud then, lifting the handles of the barrow, pushes off
manfully through the snow.

"No idea of 'effect,' no martyr-spirit or taking up

* *Scientific Spirit of the Age*, by Frances Power Cobbe.

his cross, no big talk about his self-sacrifice ; but as the Christ who became a little child, and taught us the ' inasmuch,' looked down and noticed this little street Arab—common in our London as the sparrow that He spoke of long ago—how do you think He felt about it ? And whereabouts in value do you think an action like this would come ? "

In the following we have another instance of the unselfishness of a little child. Kathie, three years old, being always very loth to part with anything she possessed, was much troubled and fearful at her mother's illness and possible death, but found it in her heart to say :—" I shouldn't like my dear mother to die, but—yet—I *should* like her to go to the golden city."

Crying.

Tears are familiar—and yet they have their mystery. Keble says :—

> Why should we faint and fear to live alone,
>   Since all alone, so Heaven has will'd, we die ?
> Nor e'en the tenderest heart, and such our own,
>   Knows half the reasons why we smile and sigh.
>
> Each in his hidden sphere of joy or woe
>   Our hermit spirits dwell and range apart,
> Our eyes see all around in gloom or glow—
>   Hues of their own, fresh borrowed from the heart.

What is that which gives most early expression to the mental states or feelings of an infant ? It is not verbal utterance, for the use of language indicates considerable progress in mental development.

Before it has acquired the power of appreciating a definite sound, or become capable of perceiving an object external to itself, its consciousness has been awakened, and has probably revealed itself to more than one person. Twenty-four hours of its life will not have passed without its making its wants or its troubles known. It soon makes use of the universal language of earliest infancy—the expressive voice of pain or of grief, and, such is the marvellous gamut of human feeling, of joy and laughter. There is a two-fold appeal, awaking inquiring sympathy as it falls upon the ear of the listener, and also to the eye, as it takes shape in a falling tear.

A tear! moulded into shape by the same forces as those which give form to the planets in their orbits; a tear for which Nature has carefully provided its appropriate receptacles, its adapted channels, and for the discharge of its valuable functions, ever delicate in its attentions to the eye, and equally resourceful and helpful for the burdened heart with its sorrows and distresses.

How deep and subtile is the sympathy evinced in the entire facial expression with the bitter tear. What contortions, what convulsive movements of the eyebrows, and of the muscles which play around the mouth!

How strange the contrast between the placid face of

contentment, and the streaming eye and the tortured countenance; and all this as strongly marked in a little child as in an adult. Indeed, there is a sense of shame and of weakness in an adult, which prompts the attempt to conceal that, which in the case of a child, is felt to be like the very profusion of eloquence.

There is nothing more demonstrative than tears. Tears command an immense variety of expression in connection with muscular contortions of the face. The elevation or depression of lips, or eyebrows, the wrinkles that overspread the countenance, and contract the smooth muscles of the forehead, like the disturbance of the fitful breeze across the placid surface of the lake.

The mobility of the features renders them ready exponents of grief or sorrow, of vexation and disappointment, of rage and anger, particularly with flowing tears. It is not less remarkable that painful and overwhelming physical sensations equally find expression through the same media. They thus become our guardians and protectors in danger, and are full of warning.

Harold was two years old, when running with his sister round the table, both fell down and were hurt. Harold ceased crying first, and, taking up his pinafore, wiped Lucy's eyes, and soon both were happy.

" Don't give me your cold," said Papa. " No," replied Harold, " I won't if I can help it ; I have just finished watering my eyes."

Children very early learn the power of tears as a means of getting what they desire. They thus acquire a commercial value and degrade the child.

A little boy sat on the floor crying. After a while he stopped, and seemed buried in thought. Looking up suddenly he said, " Mamma, what was I crying about ? " " Because I wouldn't let you go out to play." " O yes," and he set up another howl.

Genius—its early indications.

John Flaxman, the sculptor, at the age of five, was fond of examining the seals of every watch he saw, whether belonging to friend or stranger, and kept a bit of soft wax ready to take an impression of any specimen which pleased him. While yet a child he made a great number of small models, in plaster-of-Paris, wax, or clay, some of which are still preserved, and have considerable merit. At the age of eleven and five months he gained his first prize from the Society for the Encouragement of Arts, &c. At thirteen, another ; and the following year he was admitted a student at the Royal Academy, then newly established, and the same year he received their silver medal.

The calculating boy.

In an address which George Bidder delivered before the Institute of Civil Engineers of which he became the President in 1860, he endeavoured to account to his audience for the success which had attended his career, and this he attributed to the fact that he had devoted himself as a child to mental arithmetic. Beginning with ten, and going on by tens, the child soon acquired an intelligent apprehension of the meaning of 100.

His father was a working mason, near to whose house there lived a kind-hearted old blacksmith, with whom little George became acquainted, and there he was allowed to amuse himself to his heart's content. As he grew in strength he was able to blow the blacksmith's bellows, and on winter evenings little George would be perched on a seat near the forge, often listening to the old man's stories. On such occasions neighbours would drop in and listen, and one day someone seems by chance to have asked for an answer to a certain arithmetical problem, whereupon the boy without hesitation gave the correct answer to the astonishment of all present. Other questions followed, and their increasing difficulty necessitated his interrogator to resort to a board and a bit of chalk. His remarkable power soon brought him before the public as " the calculating boy." Eventually he became an engineer,

D

and a friend of George Stephenson. George Bidder died in 1878, leaving behind him many engineering works, monuments of his skill and success.

Literary.

Thomas Arnold, of Rugby, at the age of *three*, received a present of Smollett's *Historical Works*, as a reward for his accuracy in recounting the stories connected with the reigns of the Kings of England. Before he had reached his seventh year he had composed a tragedy.

Robertson, the historian, began life at fifteen with his motto—*Vita sine literis mors est.*

Preaching proclivities.

Many a celebrated preacher, like Dr. Chalmers, has preached as a child at three years of age.

Little Harold in his grandpapa's garden was overheard reading Rev. i. 1, and seen to look up and say:—" Now I wonder if any one in this congregation knows what that means."

A child who subsequently became an eminent minister and professor at a college, began preaching at the age of three, when he took for his text:—"Learn to do evil, cease to do well," at which his father remarked:—" Come, come, John, that is bad doctrine."

More reliable was the doctrine preached by John Ruskin, who began his career as a pulpit orator at the age of three with the appeal to his audience:—" Be dood people, be dood."

Curiosity and discovery.

" The holy philosopher hath said expressly that the glory of God is to conceal a thing, but the glory of the king is to find it out; as if the divine nature according to the innocent and sweet play of children which hide themselves to the end that they may be found, took delight to hide His works, to the end they might be found out ; and, of His indulgence and goodness to mankind, had chosen the soul of man to be His play-fellow in this game."*

Lessing's answer to the question :—" If *truth* were held out to him in one hand, and search of the truth in the other hand, the philosopher's choice would, as a rule, be the answer of the child." The process of *investigation* affords keener interest, and stimulates greater curiosity and wonder, than the actual posses-sion of the thing sought. " I want to know " is the indication of a healthy activity.

How often, however, is inquiry repressed and even stifled ? " Why are they called sisters of mercy, mamma ? " " That's a name they have given to them," says the unappreciative parent.

* Bacon's *De Augmentis.*

D 2

"Little children must not ask questions," says another foolish parent, not knowing that little children are born notes of interrogation.

H. S. was an original inquirer. Before he was four years old he studied the alphabet by his mother's side, and commenced putting letters together and forming words by his unassisted application. He was interested at a very early period in the study of geography and geology. His apprehension of the spirituality of God was drawn forth by a scripture text, " Thou, God, seest me."

In many instances, far from encouragement being given to a child to pursue the bent of its genius, the child has succeeded in spite of the difficulties and the opposition it has had to contend with.

Blaise Pascal, from his earliest childhood, discovered a remarkable aptitude for mathematics. Geometry therefore was kept out of his sight, lest it should interfere with his appointed studies. Nevertheless, the force of his genius discovered the elementary truths of the forbidden science. When he was twelve years old his father found him in the act of demonstrating a problem on the pavement of an old hall where he used to play. A rough diagram, traced with a piece of coal, was found to be a proposition corresponding to the thirty-second proposition of the first book of Euclid. Other discoveries are recorded, following on the earlier unfolding of his remarkable mind.

How a little girl suggested the invention of the telescope.

Nearly three hundred years ago, there was living in the town of Middleburg, on the island of Walcheren, in the Netherlands, a poor optician, named Hans Lippersheim. One day, in the year 1608, he was working in his shop, his children helping him in various small ways, or romping about and amusing themselves with the tools and objects lying on his workbench, when suddenly his little girl exclaimed:—" Oh, Papa! see how near the steeple comes!" Half startled by this announcement, the honest Hans looked up from his work, curious to know the cause of the child's amazement.

Turning towards her, he saw that she was looking through two lenses, one held close to her eye, and the other at arm's length; and, calling his daughter to his side, he noticed that the eye-lens was plano-concave (or flat on one side and hollowed out on the other), while the one held at a distance was plano-convex (or flat on one side and bulging on the other).

Then, taking the two glasses, he repeated his daughter's experiment, and soon discovered that she had chanced to hold the lenses apart at their exact focus, and this had produced the wonderful effect that she had observed. His quick wit and skilled invention saw in this accident a wonderful discovery.

He immediately set about making use of his knowledge of lenses, and ere long he had fashioned a pasteboard tube, in which he set the glasses firmly at their exact focus.

This rough tube was the germ of the great instrument, the telescope, to which modern science owes so much; and it was on October 22nd, 1608, that Lippersheim sent to his government three telescopes made by himself, calling them "instruments by means of which to see at a distance."

The discovery of the stethoscope.

Laennec, the eminent French physician, related to one of his friends the story of his discovery. Walking through the court of the Louvre, he observed some children amusing themselves by holding a cylindrical piece of wood to the ear and scratching with a pin on the further end of it. Thereby they produced a noise louder than the scratching of a pin produces under ordinary circumstances. Next morning visiting his patients in the Hospital Necker, he extemporised a hollow cylinder out of a roll of paper, and applied it over the heart of one of the patients. This was his first stethoscope.

, Raphael's first playthings were the implements of his father's art, and the latter delighted on all occasions to encourage tendencies which seemed the presage of an extraordinary vocation to the noble art he himself so loved.*

* De Quincey's *Lives of M. Angelo and Raphael.*

Boy inventors.

Some of the most important inventions have been the work of mere boys. The invention of the valve motion to the steam engine was made by a boy, Humphrey Potter, in 1713. The steam-engine at that date was in a very incomplete condition from the fact that there was no method of opening or closing the valve of the cylinder, except by means of levers operated by the hand.

One of Newcomen's engines being at work at one of the mines, a boy was hired to work the valve-levers. Although this was not hard work, yet it required his constant attention. As the boy, Potter, was working these levers, he saw that parts of the engine moved in the right direction, and at the exact time that he had to open or close the valves. He procured a strong cord, and made one end fast to the proper part of the engine, and the other end to the valve-lever. Then he had the satisfaction of seeing the engine work with perfect regularity of motion.

A short time after, the foreman came round, and saw the boy playing marbles at the door. Looking at the engine, he soon perceived the ingenuity of the boy, and also the advantages of so great a discovery. Some few years later, Henry Beighton, in 1718, worked out the boy's invention in a practical form, making the steam-engine a perfect automatic working machine.

James Watt, almost the inventor of the steam-engine, was a very weakly child. He early manifested a turn for mathematics and calculations, and took a great interest in machines.

The power-loom is the invention of a farmer-boy, who had never seen or heard of such a thing. He cut one out with his knife, and after he had got it all done, he, with great enthusiasm, showed it to his father, who at once kicked it to pieces, saying he would have no boy about him that would spend his time on such foolish things.

The boy was afterwards apprenticed to a blacksmith, and he soon found that his new master was kind, and took a lively interest in him. He had made a loom of what was left of the one his father had broken up, which he showed to his master. The blacksmith saw that he had no common boy as an apprentice, and that the invention was a very valuable one.

He immediately had a loom constructed, under the supervision of the boy. It worked to their perfect satisfaction, and the blacksmith furnished the means to manufacture the looms, the boy to receive one-half the profits.

In about a year the blacksmith wrote to the boy's father that he should visit him and bring with him a wealthy gentleman who was the inventor of the celebrated power-loom.

Judge of the astonishment at the old home, when the son was presented by the blacksmith as the inventor, who told the father that the loom was the same as the model that he had kicked to pieces but a year before.

Smeaton, the great mechanic, when a boy, disdained the ordinary playthings of boyhood, collecting the tools of workmen whom he bothered with no end of questions. One day, after having watched some mill-wrights, he was discovered, to the great distress of his family, in a situation of extreme danger, fixing a wind-mill on the top of the barn. His father sent him to London to study law ; but he declared that "law did not suit the bent of his genius," and addressed a memorial to his father to show his utter incompetency for legal pursuits. His father acted wisely, and finally allowed him to do as he wished. It was he who built the Eddystone light-house.

The young musician.

Wolfgang Amadeus Mozart, the great composer, in infancy listened to his sister's playing on the harpsi-chord with intense delight ; and at the age of *four* his father gave him lessons every day, and in his fifth year he began to compose melodies. He was taken, at the age of six, on a tour with his sister for the exhibition of their musical talents, and at a Franciscan convent in Austria, he surprised the monks by the taste and skill with which he played the organ.

Imitation.

Harold (four) dressed himself up in rugs, and stuffed a towel in front of him; "There," he said to his mother, "see my dress improver, mamma; I'm a lady like you."

Memory.

When Dr. Johnson was a child in petticoats, and had learned to read, his mother put the Common Prayer book into his hands, pointing to the collect for the day, and said, "Sam, you must get this by heart." She went upstairs leaving him to study it, but by the time she had reached the second floor she heard him following her." What's the matter?" she asked. "I can say it," he replied, and repeated it distinctly, though he could not have read it more than twice.

Punning.

Tom Hood may have punned in his cradle, even in his babyhood. The following of a little girl of three years is authentic. Being asked if she understood the phrase in the nursery rhyme of the maiden *all forlorn* that milked the cow with the crumpled horn, said, "Oh yes, I know it means, not get your feet wet on the grass, *off the lawn.*"

Muriel when five years of age remarked to her mother when her father was travelling in Spain :—
" It's very lonely for dear father in Barcelona without his wife, perhaps that is why it is called Barce-*lona*."

Precocity and dulness.

Precocity has its marvels, but it has its dangers, and sometimes it forebodes premature decay. Bishop Hall wrote :—" I never dared hope much from those great beginnings of intellect and of memory which are nevertheless so much admired in children. I know well that a child must first come to his strength, and if those things that are proper to a later age show themselves earlier, he is not the better for it."

Social precocity.

Percy (eleven) :—" It is easy enough for me to love the young ladies, but not so easy to get them to love me."

Ernest (five), one day walking home from school with a little girl, afterwards met one of his father's friends, who pretended to be surprised that he should walk with her, as he thought he preferred the society of gentlemen. " So I do," said Ernest, " but the ladies like a man."

*Intellectual precocity compatible with goodness and sim-
plicity of heart.*

Of the boyhood of Lord Macaulay, his mother
wrote :—

" He gets on wonderfully in all branches of his
education, and the extent of his reading, and the
knowledge he has derived from it, are truly astonishing
in a boy not yet eight years old. He is at the same
time as playful as a kitten."

Dullness.

Dr. Thomas Fuller remarks :—" Hard, rugged, and
dull natures of youth acquit themselves afterwards and
become the jewels of the country, and therefore their
dullness at first is to be borne with if they are diligent.
That schoolmaster deserves to be beaten himself *who
beats Nature* in a boy for a fault. And I question
whether all the whipping in the world can make their
parts which are naturally sluggish, rise one minute
before the hour Nature hath appointed."

Destructive or constructive ?

Toys or playthings are the means by which the
child-investigator enquires into the structure of things;
and the pleasure of investigation is not fully attained
till the toy is pulled to pieces. " What's in the

drum ? " is the great question of the enquiring mind. True, a great many toys go to a complete demonstration. But give the children toys of construction, and see what busy and successful builders they will become.

Reason.

A child's earliest conception of God must needs be inadequate, incomplete, and often grotesque. Its intuitions of a transcending love and power will probably be much nearer the truth, than any formal representation of God which its little mind may have imaged. The ideas thus conceived may be very natural. They are readily traceable in the analogies of father and offspring, but the details of such an analogy are often very intractable, and not easily adjusted. The following instance is to the point.

Babs, three years old.

Mother : " Good night, baby, God bless you."

B. : " What is God ? "

M. : " Oh ! Our Heavenly Father, you know."

B. : " Oh ! I see ; a Dadda that never comes down to breakfast."

Babs' acquaintance with her father being limited to the breakfast-table, she holds him in great contempt if at any time he has not put in an appearance at that meal.

Enid (four) being anxious to go and take part in a funeral she was watching from the house opposite, was told that they were only taking away the body of the lady, the angels having previously fetched her spirit home. A few days later Enid looked wistfully again at the house, and said :—" If I ask very gently, do you think they would let me go and see that lady's arms and legs ; they must look very interesting lying on the bed alone."

Babs (two and a half), and Enid (four and a half), modelling in clay from a pea-pod. B. : " Enid, did God make this pea ? " E. : " Yes, Babs, God makes everything." B. (pulling a maggot out of one of the peas) : " He didn't make much of a one of this, did He, Enid ? "

Another story, on the same authority, supplies a singular example of theological reasoning.

Enid and Babs in bed Christmas eve.

B. : " Enid, does God give us all our toys ? thought it was Father Christmas ! "

E. (in explanatory tone) : " But God tells the reindeers what chimneys to stop at."

B. : " He must know a great deal to tell all that."

E. (reflectively) : " What did they do when God was in Jesus, because there was no God in the sky to keep the people in the world good."

There was no irreverence in these little children, who in their simplicity were true to the very little they had been taught, and as they were never left to servants for an hour, it seems as if they evolved their theological notions by themselves.

The young theologians' posers.—" Mother," said a child between three and four, " when God was having the flood, why did'nt he drown the Devil too ? "

Gertrude (same age) : " Why didn't He make them all good, then ? "

Reasoning.

Practical logician—George, a little boy of five: " Mother, have I been good lately ? " " I think you have." " Oh well, I shall leave off praying now, for it is no use asking God to make me good, if I am good."

Another day he asked :—" Mother, have you done growing yet ? " " Yes ? then you can't grow any better than you are ? "

Reasoning from inadequate data—" Mother, who was my mother when you were a little girl ? "

Faculty of comparison.—A boy of six drew his mother's attention to a fly which was contemplating a drop of juice upon the table ; he remarked that to the fly that drop of water was a large pond.

Little Harold : " I suppose God learned to do these clever things when He was a little boy."

His analogical reasoning :—" Papa, do you think the birds play hide and seek, when they call cuckoo ? "

On another occasion, during breakfast and while eating eggs and bacon :—" Grandma, do fowls lay bacon ? " After asking how old the world was and being told it was supposed to be many thousands of years old before Adam was created, he said:—"Oh! what a lot of weeds there must have been; Adam must have had enough to do to clear them all away."

A little child at two and a half years, on catching pussy in the act of stealing some milk, reproved her thus:—"You're a very naughty pussy; I can't love you and Jesus can't love you, at least not very much."

The logic of the stomach,—Mabel (seven and a half), Christmas morning:—"We had better not eat no brekner"—so as to be better prepared for grandma's Christmas dinner.

A boy called on the nurse for help for his mother, "who had had a new baby." *Nurse:* "And how old is mother's new baby?" *Small boy:* "Oh; we don't know yet, mother only had it on Sunday." The logic of this seems to be that the age of a baby is to be determined by internal evidence as the age of a tree by its rings.

Child's compliment to his mother :—

John (aged six) was particularly fond of Roman and Grecian history; he had a great veneration for his mother, and was astonished one day to find that she did not know everything.

The same lady was once a governess in a family, and her pupil was surprised that she was not encyclopædic. In her indignation the child went to her father and told him that the governess was not fit to teach her as she did not know everything. The father smiled and opened his child's eyes a little wider when he told her that he was in the same hapless condition.

Mabel (five) : "Mamma, do you love God ? Then I shall love him if you do."

The heroism of childhood.

On the morning of the third day out from Liverpool, a young stowaway was discovered among the casks for'ard, in a ship bound for New York. He was "a little bit of a lad" not ten years old—ragged as a scarecrow, but with a bright little face, only fearfully thin and pale.

He stood before the first mate on the forecastle, surrounded by crew and passengers.

"What brought you here?" asked the first mate grimly.

"It was my step-father as done it," said the child, in a feeble but steady voice. "Father's dead and mother's married again, and my new father says as how he won't have us brats about eatin' up his wages, and he stowed me away when nobody wer'n't lookin' and gave me some grub to keep me goin' for a day or two till I got to sea"; and he pulled out a dirty bit of paper with the address of an aunt to whom he was to go.

The sailors believed the boy, but the first mate was incredulous.

"Look here, my lad," said he ; "that's all very

E

fine but it won't do *here*. Now point out the man who stowed and fed you, or it will be the worse for you."

The boy looked with a bright and fearless face, and in a firm voice said, " I've told you the truth."

" Heave a rope to the yard. Smart now," commanded the mate.

The men looked at one another in surprise, but they obeyed.

The rope ready, the mate said to the little lad :— " Now, my lad, you see that rope. I'll give you ten minutes to confess," and he took out his watch and held it in his hand, " and if you do not tell the truth before the time is up, I'll hang you like a dog."

A sullen growl of remonstrance passed round among the men.

" Silence there," cried the mate. And with his own hands he put the noose round the boy's neck. The little fellow never flinched, but some of the sailors shook with excitement.

" Eight minutes," shouted the mate ; " if you have anything to confess, you'd best out with it, for your time's nearly up."

" I've told you the truth," answered the boy, very pale but quite unmoved, " and I cannot tell a lie. May I say my prayers, please ? "

The mate nodded, and the little fellow went down on his knees with the rope still round his neck. And putting his hands together he softly repeated the prayers he had learned from his mother's lips. Then rising, and folding his hands behind him, he said to the mate, very softly, " I'm ready."

The hard heart of the mate broke. He snatched the child up in his arms, kissed him and wept over him. "God bless you, my boy; you would not tell a lie to save your life. I will be a father to you." And the mate kept his word.

James Bristow, a boy of eight years, lived with his mother at Walthamstow. Mrs. Bristow went out on an errand, leaving the boy in charge of the little three-year old sister. A small parafin-lamp was burning in a corner of the room, and to reach it the child climbed upon a chair, and upset the lamp. The parafin caught fire and the child's dress was quickly in flames. The boy might have run off in terror to find his mother; but he tore off the child's garments, and put her on the bed. In doing so, his own clothes caught fire, and it took the poor boy some time to tear them off. He succeeded at last, but he was so seriously hurt that, though taken at once to the hospital, the injuries proved fatal within a week.

Is it too much to say that the presence of mind, the self-command, the fortitude of this little boy, and above all his self-obliviousness, afford a glimpse of that spiritual element of life which implies a Divine source ?

An act of heroism in an adult is often prompted by love of praise. A man does not like to be thought a coward, and he is stimulated by a sense of public opinion. A child, like James Bristow, is not worldly-minded enough to be swayed by such considerations.

Glory and honour.

" My story begins at the moment when the prizes are given. Now fancy the scene. The Earl (Lord Shaftesbury) rises. The table is piled up with articles, and certain boys approach one by one. First comes the winner of the prize for punctuality. Every boy behind had had his chance at it, and there stands the boy that has won it. He takes an accordion away, and goes back to his seat while cheers rise from every quarter of the hall, but chiefly from the five hundred throats and five hundred pairs of clapping hands of his young vanquished competitors. You could scarcely believe it possible that anything awaited other boys to be compared in triumphant joy with this. Then comes the prize for writing. Its winner advances to the front and receives it. At this, all the little fellows there, who had themselves been leaning over their desks, sitting on their bare-board forms, with their pens in their hands, dipping them in ink-pots just above, and their two big serious eyes fixed on the words between the lines in their copy-books, steadily making it true to the copy there—yes, all of them, with one accord, broke out afresh in a glorious uproar, and the boy that had beaten them

all carried off a desk. Next came the thrift prize for
the boy who had spent the least of his pocket money,
and saved the most in his box. His thrift might have
been the act of self-denial, but I fear it had in it some
element of meanness, for the cheers lost a little of their
swing. Others came, and as each carried off his prize
hands and voices fell to clapping and shouting, and
hearts seemed to bound and sing. Then the next boy
came. Suddenly all the joy went out of the place as
light goes when the gas is put out. And there was
a dead silence. To everybody it seemed as if something was going to happen. The whole place became
almost breathless. What was the matter? What we
saw was a little figure standing at one end of the table,
evidently timid, and screwing up his courage, for he was
very pale and had put out his fingers on to the edge of
the table, as it would seem to steady himself. The Earl
said, 'I have now the honour—,' and he paused, and
drew himself up, as if making room for a great swell of
feeling, at the same time lifting something from the
table almost reverently (it was a little box). He opened it, and took into his hand a small round medal.
The audience at each second became stiller and with
almost distressing suspense ; and, to catch every word
that was to be spoken, it became stillness itself. The
Earl continued in a subdued tone, 'This boy has
saved life!' That boy? A something went right
through the place. The audience could restrain itself
no longer, and broke out in tumultuous cheers again

and again, hands and feet and voices. Handkerchiefs were waved, and hundreds of strong men were in tears. Meanwhile the Earl was pinning a medal on the child's jacket, and the child himself was lifting the hand he had put out to the table, and drawing the back of it across his eyes. He could save life, it seemed, but he could not stand praise, and he quietly sidled away. But his comrades behind the chair would not allow that. They gave great cries of 'hurrahs,' which quivered with feelings that had been in no shouts before, standing on the seats, and looking over one anothers' heads. And the boys who had won the writing-desks and accordions, as he went by, put them down and clapped him on the back. He had undoubtedly done better than they all."

"Now, those lads felt something of the grand sacred feeling with which all heaven casts down its crowns, and shouts the supreme triumphant glory of Jesus; for that boy had in him some of the glory sacred with the sanctity of God, and which all creatures were made to do homage to, the glory which is the especial glory of the Saviour of the world."*

Prejudice.

The prejudice of a child is not always deep-rooted.

"A gentle-looking girl of about six years of age,

* *Address to Children on Glory and Honour*, by Rev. Benjamin Waugh, Oct. 1883.

whose father was a much-respected European, and
whose mother was an Arab, surprised me very much
one day, by saying in Arabic, without any provocation,
and with a gesture of scorn, to a Jewish workman,
' Go, thou Jew, and be crucified.' The child naturally
good-natured and affectionate, shuddered when she
partially understood how cruel and unjust her words
were. By my wish, she begged pardon of the Jew,
and then, by her own impulse, and to his great
wonder, kissed his hands, while tears stood in her
eyes."*

Social distinctions, rank, &c.

Nothing can be clearer than the New Testament
teaching on the question of rank—of social position—
in relation to the kingdom which is "not of this
world." The brother of low degree is to rejoice in
his exaltation, and the brother of high degree is to
triumph over the accidents of birth, and to rejoice
that he finds himself on an equally grand footing as
the humblest in this world's estimate.

Does childhood forecast this "equality" of the Kingdom? Was the child that Jesus took and set in the
midst of His disciples the child of a prince or of a
peasant? The question is out of place. It was *a
child*, and the child was to be regarded as stripped of
all accidents of birth and parentage. The *ideal* child

* Rogers' *Domestic Life in Palestine*, p. 189.

was represented by the particular specimen that happened to be at hand.

The friend to whom this suggestion was first made
remarked that it was all very well to speak of poverty
as a blessing and to look with interest on a *poor* child,
but that wealth even for children had its advantages ;
but he did not quite realize the position. It is not a
question of wealth or poverty. Either may be a
temptation and a curse. But both are the *accidents*
and not the *essentials* of a man or child.

But here is the charm of the point. The child, as
such, is unconscious of what is regarded as the social
degradation of its poverty ; or, if born to wealth, is
uninfluenced by the habits of thought and feeling engendered by wealth. The spirituality of the child's
nature has, as yet, received none of the lights and
shadows of poverty and riches, and everyone has probably had opportunity of noticing the fraternizing of
two children coming from opposite ranks of life. The
accidents are overlooked ; the essentials are recognized.
The children are *brothers*, and they have, as yet, no
social distinction to restrain them. On the one side
there is no pride to assert itself ; on the other, no
shame to hide, and thus they will play together in the
streets of their Jerusalem.

The Christian "*world*" may get some help and
guidance from such little children.

When he was a boy, the late Prince Imperial of
France left the Tuileries one day for a ramble, having

been seized with a strong desire to go and join some boys who were snow-balling. He returned after an absence of about four hours, to find his parents in the utmost agitation as to what had become of him. The little King of Rome, Napoleon the First's son, once wanted to play truant in the same way, but was checked in time. He then declared with many tears, that he wanted to go and make mud-pies with some dirty boys who were playing on the quays of the Seine.

Childhood unmoral.

"Because man cannot succeed in poising himself against Nature, it does not follow that he cannot take her hand and be lifted to her level. But this would be his becoming *unmoral*, as a little child. (Here, perhaps, is where the precepts of Christ have appeared unpractical or impossible. We have not noticed this basis of them all. He is supposing men to have accepted the becoming as a little child). We have not recognized this element in being raised to the level of *Nature*, and have sought it, if at all, combined with our morality. The question is:—Is Nature infra-moral or super-moral?"*

"When we know that exactly in proportion as a man is more a man and worthier, so are things not evil to him, which are evil to those less worthy, and when we know, too, that Christ set a little child as His pattern, to whom *things* are not evil."†

* Hinton's *Law-Breaker*, p. 299.   † *Ibid.*, p. 300.

"The advance comes through the children. The difficulty of the grown-up men and women is not that they cannot take up the new right, but that they cannot let go the old. But this latter has not to be done by the children at all. The change is in two portions, one hard, the other not hard. Now, the children have only one of these to do, that which is not hard ; the hard one does not come to them."*

A boy of five years sometimes asked his father troublesome questions, but his father gave him an answer in long, hard words that the child had never heard; but George would never acknowledge that he did not understand, and answered on such occasions, "Thank you, I see."

May we not hope that in this case there was not so much a false assumption of knowledge as a loving desire to appreciate the father's kind but doubtfully wise explanation ?

Unmoral.—Little boy wearied with school tasks sighed :—" Oh, if all the world would but agree to *know* a little less !"†

Explanations.—Ernest (five). One day he asked where the old moons went to. Nurse tried to explain to him that it was the same moon, but he was sure there must be old ones if there were new ones. Presently he said :—" I'll tell you where the old ones go to, they drop down behind the clouds, and the new ones spring out of the clouds, the same as crocuses do out of the earth."

      * *Ibid.*, p. 302.   † *Parent's Review*, Jan. 1894.

Do we understand and trust our children ?

" I once had a boy, the son of a Methodist minister,
—you would think a minister ought to understand
his boy. This boy came to my school. His father
thought he was converted. . . . . . His father brought
him to me and said, ' I want you to take this boy ; he
is very bad, but I can do nothing with him. You do
a very good work here ; I should like you to try him.'
I looked into the boy's face. There was a talismanic
(that is not the right word, but it will do) look passed
between him and myself, and I thought I could do
something with him. There came a time when it
was necessary to decide as to the truthfulness of this
boy. The teacher brought certain charges which the
boy denied. The teacher did not understand the
character he was dealing with, but I felt certain that
the boy's story was straight, and when the charges
had been made, I said to the boy ' State your case.'
And when he was through I said, ' I believe you.'
The boy burst into tears. He did not know what
to say. Why, it was the first 'time in his life that
he had found somebody who absolutely believed
him. He turned all kinds of colours. He went to
his seat and I dismissed the teacher. The boy came
into my office a few minutes afterwards, and took me
by the hand, still sobbing. He said, ' Mr. Packard, I
will never do a bad thing again in your school, as long

as I live.' I said ' Why ? ' ' Because you believe I told the truth, and I did tell the truth ; and I am going to show that I deserve the confidence.'

" In a week his father came to see me. He walked up to me and said, ' You have given me a son, and I want to thank you.' I said ' I don't understand.' He answered, ' I didn't know my own boy. I thought him converted, but he was not. You converted him ; he is the talk of the neighbourhood ; he cannot think anything wrong ; he cannot do anything wrong." *

Christian portraiture anticipated in a little child.

See his clear large eyes : mark his plump cheeks : no wrinkles on his brow : no lines of thought. Do you charge him with carelessness, with thoughtlessness ?

What did Jesus say to His disciples ? *" Take no thought for the morrow ! "* " Be careful for nothing ! " O blessed childhood !

Receptivity.

" Except ye receive the kingdom of heaven as a little child ye shall in no wise enter therein."

Here, the knowledge of the nature of a little child— the nature possessed by our Lord—served Him with a striking illustration. It was not easy to convey to His disciples a true conception of His kingdom. But a little child might help them.

* *Parent's Review*, Nov. 1893.

What is that in a little child which commends itself as a feature one would like to reflect?

We are familiar with such explanations as are usually given; such as the child's 'humility,' 'simplicity,' &c.; but our Lord tells us in the shortest possible way what He means. He says the kingdom of heaven is to be *received*; and thus we get the very attitude of mind necessary to its reception.

The receptivity of a child is much greater in early or in earliest years than afterwards. It is as yet more passive than active. It is now susceptible of unfading *impressions*, for earliest impressions are most ineradicable. The child's mind has no *preoccupations*.

Place the child in relation with any object it has not before observed. It is quiet, its activities are completely arrested. For its little mind receiving and absorbing impressions, impressions reaching its mind through the senses, wonder, admiration, fear, curiosity and other feelings are awakened. The child is acted upon, it is not acting. The activities are aroused in due course.

Our Lord says that to enter into the Kingdom, a man must become a little child. He receives, and by means of his receiving he enters.

The narrative in Mark's Gospel (x. 13—17), is followed by the story of the young man who came running to Christ, and who asked Him the question, "What shall I do that I may inherit eternal life?" Our Lord knew and at once revealed the man to himself. He was not a child. Alas! all the avenues to his receptive faculties were choked up with hard cash. "He was very rich." His soul was pre-occupied, "and he went away sad." He had too much to carry. He would not become a receptive little child. He was too full to receive the kingdom of heaven.

Another glimpse of the Master's intimate knowledge of human nature is brought to our mind in what follows: "I thank thee, O Father, that Thou hast hid these things from the wise and prudent, and hast revealed them unto *babes*."

Here we have the two great obstacles to the reception of the kingdom of heaven. One of these is represented by the rich young man, the type of worldly-mindedness, and heart-absorption in wealth; the other is found in human philosophy, and usually in a theologic form.

A little child is free from both these forms of entanglement and spiritual destruction. It is destitute of earthly possessions; therefore it is capable of receiving. It has no notions in its head; therefore it has no difficulties of belief. The heart is free. The mind is free. Men and women must empty themselves of self in all its forms, in order to be receptive. Thus they become once more little children. This is only another way of saying "Ye must be born again," is it not?

It is its receptivity that makes a little child so charming.

Filial affection and God's Heaven.

" A boy of six years named Tommy Lloyd, son of Mr. James Lloyd, residing in the mountain hamlet of Meingwynionmawr, was missing from home during the recent snowstorm. The villagers, armed with long staves, turned out in a body to the hills, resolved to spare no effort in finding the lost child. After they had spent ten hours among the hills and valleys a messenger arrived on horseback with the news that the missing boy had safely arrived at Llwynwermwent, near Newquay, where his mother was visiting some friends. So great had been the little fellow's longing for his mother that he braved the bitter cold and blinding drifts of snow and accomplished a journey of seven miles over the bleakest uplands in Cardigan-shire." *

Ernest, aged three (to his nurse), " I should like papa and me to go to Heaven ; " then followed rapidly a list of his relations who were to go there too, ending with, " How happy we'll all be when God is ready for us."

Faithfulness.

" In Mr. Giammal's establishment there were several black servants,—good-natured Abyssinian girls. They looked very picturesque in their holiday dresses. One

* *Daily News,* Jan. 16, 1893.

day there was great rejoicing among them, and cries of congratulation echoed throughout the house. I inquired the cause. I found that a young slave girl who had been hired by Mr. Giammal, had just been set free. She was the property of an Arab widow lady. . . . . . The poor girl was at first quite overcome with delight and wonder, but on reflection she seemed almost to tremble at the loneliness and responsibility of her new position. She asked her mistress if she could always love her just as much as she had loved her before, and added, ' I would rather keep your love than gain my freedom.'"*

What only a child can do.

Being in Brussels, I visited the Royal Lace Factory. In the *Atelier* I watched the women and girls at work on some of the finest specimens of their artistic labour. One was quite an old woman, who, in her spectacles, was still able to do a full day's work, at which she contentedly earned two francs a day. She had been at it over forty years. Sight, as a rule, goes much sooner.

"And how old are they when they begin to learn the art?" I asked; and was informed in reply that they commenced between the ages of four and five. "That is very young." "Yes, but it teaches the children the lesson of patience; and, if they did not

* Rogers' *Domestic Life in Palestine*, p. 377.

begin when young, they would never acquire the ability to do such fine work."

My informant seemed to think that *patience* was about the highest possible attainment. It is a divine virtue, but not the only one; and it is to be wished that *hope* (another great and healthy virtue), still finds a home in the hearts of these hard-working people.

But I was struck with the fact that the art must be acquired when the children are quite young, and the spirituality of the child received a new and striking illustration.

The faculties of a child are so pliant, so fresh, so clear, and the work of the Brussels lace is so fine and delicate, that the child, before its perceptions are blunted, before its tastes have become degraded, before its senses are made coarse, and before it has known anything of disobedience and discontent, takes readily to a life's devotion, whose beautiful productions adorn a princess and grace the most fashionable assemblies.

Poor little child,—have all who wear your lace as patient, as contented, as happy a life as yours?

And you can acquire what older people were incompetent to attain: and you can do what older hands were unable to perform.

Only by conversion, and becoming as little children, can the world-encrusted soul acquire once more the capacity for many a delicate and difficult spiritual acquirement.

F

The will.

There is no necessity to discuss the metaphysics of what we recognize as *Will* in a child. Its manifestation from a very early period none will dispute.

It may be observed, however, that what we trace in an uneducated adult as Will determined mainly by emotion, is strikingly evident in a child. The will is moved by emotional impulse. How can it be otherwise? Experience has as yet taught nothing; and reason is but in its dawn.

Musicians.

Infant prodigies in music were never more numerous than now. But all performers are not composers.

Among the most remarkable of child composers may be mentioned the boy Handel. As is very often the case, the genius of the child was opposed, and Handel was intended by his father for the profession of the law. But the boy got to the clavichord in an attic, with the sound so deadened, that he might follow his bent unknown to his family, and as an infant he made surpassing progress in manipulating the instrument as well as in original composition.

Mozart, at the age of five, had produced several pieces of music.

Harry at nine months would listen intelligently to

music, and at four and a half years of age he sang to a large audience, making an hour's entertainment entirely himself.

Artists and sculptors.

Sir Thomas Lawrence, at six years of age, produced excellent portraits of Lord and Lady Kenyon.

Antonio Canova, almost as soon as he could hold a pencil, was initiated into the principles of drawing; and while still a boy, worked as a sculptor and acquired fame.

A rapid awakening.

Miss Martineau tells us of a schoolboy of *ten*, who laid himself down, back uppermost, with Southey's *Thalaba* before him, on the first day of the Easter holidays, and turned over the leaves, notwithstanding his inconvenient position, as fast as if he were looking for something, till in a very few hours it was done, and he was off with it to the public library, bringing back the *Curse of Kehama*. Thus he went on with all Southey's poems, and some others, through his short holidays, scarcely moving voluntarily all those days except to run to the library. " He came out of the process so changed that none of his family could help being struck by it. The expression of his eye, the cast of his countenance, his use of words, and his very gait were changed. In ten days he had advanced years in

F 2

intelligence ; and I have always thought that this was
the turning point of his life. His parents wisely and
kindly let him alone, aware that school would presently
put an end to all excess in the new indulgence."

Scientific observation.

James Ferguson, the astronomer, was the child of
a day labourer. The day's work done, the boy went
out into the fields, where he wrapped himself in his
blanket, and lying on the grass, with a thread on which
beads were strung, measured the distances and movements of the stars.   He was taught by an old woman,
through whom he learnt the alphabet, and then to read,
much to the astonishment of his father. While yet
a boy he discovered the properties of lever and axle.
Though to him an original discovery, he was chagrined
when he subsequently found books recording the same
discovery by others.

The great Faraday became an errand boy to a bookbinder at the age of twelve. A year later he was a
bookseller's and bookbinder's apprentice.   He now
had the opportunity of making acquaintance with the
treasures of the *Encyclopædia Britannica*, Mrs. Marcet's
Conversations on Chemistry, &c.   After dipping into
these works, he came to the conclusion that it was
not his lot to be " a deep thinker or a very precocious
person," thus betraying that humility which remained
a charming element of his character throughout his
splendid career.

Manners.

Politeness. It is the custom in all good Spanish families always to leave something on one's plate, in order not to appear too great an eater. They accustom their children to this habit by telling them frequently, " Politeness requires you to leave something on your plate ; don't forget this, it is politeness." At the table where a friend of mine was sitting, a little girl two and a half years old had reluctantly left a portion of some sweet dish. She leaned towards her mother and whispered in her ear, but loud enough to be heard by everybody : — " Please mamma, may I eat politeness to-day ? "

Life and death illustrated.

Ernest (five) had been asking about his heart beat- 'ing, and after his nurse had explained it he said :— " Oh yes, I know now ; it's like my highlander ; when the top spins, he can dance ; when it stops he can't do it ; that's the difference between life and death."

The imagination and the senses.

The illusions of the senses are usually corrected by the reason ; but the following is an instance of the correction of the imagination by an appeal to the senses.

Ernest (four) went to his father's office in
Birmingham on the occasion of a visit by the Queen,
to witness the procession from the Town Hall. Hearing the cheers of the crowd, he began saying to himself
the lines of Mrs. Crewdson from *The Martyrdom of
Marius* :—

> " And the clamours of the people
>   Through the Arch of Titus roll,
> All down the Roman Forum
>   To the towering Capitol."

Ernest was grievously disappointed not to see the
Queen in her crown and robes, and remarked, " She's
only a stout old lady with grey hair."

Children are original, but they are sometimes apt at
quotation as witness the following :—

Ernest (under three) on his father's return from a
tour in Scotland, expressed his delight as he followed
him into his room, in the following quotation from
" The Spider and the Fly :"

> " Dear friend, what can I do,
>   To prove the warm affection
> I always felt for you ? "

At three he could repeat many of Lear's *Nonsense
Rhymes*. The river Thames was pointed out to him.
The passengers on the steamer were much amused
when he at once repeated :

> " There was an old person of Ems,
>   Who casually fell in the Thames,
>   But when he was found,
>   They said he was drowned,
>   This silly old person of Ems."

. And at four he remarked, " My papa isn't like the busy bee ; the bee improves the shining hour, but my papa improves it whether the sun shines or not."

Democracy among the children.

Is childhood affected by the democratic spirit of the age ?

Madge, a little girl, went into the fields one day with a lady who took her camp-stool. The lady had sat down by a field of mangolds. After a little time Madge proposed that her friend should now stand while she took the stool. It was suggested to Madge that she should sit on a mangold. Madge tried first one and then another, but with the same result—she tumbled off them all. A broad hint to the lady that she should now try the mangolds and let Madge have the stool.

Muriel, at two and a half years, was discovered in proud possession of a hammer and some tacks, and on being deprived of the same by her grandmother indignantly flung after her retreating form the rebuke— " Don't be selfish grandma !"

The preceding facts and observations have been selected, as far as possible, not for the purpose of showing what a child thinks and does under the most favourable conditions of early training, but what the child must be, and what it will do, apart from previous experience and anterior to the time which brings guidance or promptings from without.

Material, either objective or subjective, upon which the little one may exercise its faculties, must present itself to the mind, and appropriate stimuli to the formation of purpose must rouse the imagination. As much as this there must be. The infant is utterly unequal to an *a priori* assumption. But more than this would interfere with the child's individuality, and its unbiassed action. Its mental conceptions would cease to be original ; and our surprise would vanish when we knew that decisions arrived at under the direct influence of its surroundings and the suggestions offered to the infant by its attendants, had been impressed on the child's mind.

We want to see, with the *minimum* of personal experience, and a will unbiassed from without, how the infant will behave. It will now form its own conceptions of its little bit of mental property, and it will make its own experiments upon it ; and when it gives utterance to its ideas we may get, what we may fairly expect, an original observation. And we are continually amused and surprised at the strange conclusions at which the child has arrived. We pronounce him clever. We are astonished ; but our astonishment is often due to our failing to notice that the child could come to no other conclusion from the premises than that which it had reached. Its facts were really most simple, and its induction the

most slender. Its startling conclusion was really inevitable. We are surprised at the child's originality,
because his standpoint differs so widely from ours
owing to our mental training and varied experience.
Our course of thought and the determining factors
of our action, are based upon the training which has
for years been going on in our natures and characters.

The interest and value, therefore, of instances adduced in the foregoing pages, must be estimated by the
degree of freedom from restraint on the one hand, and
on the other hand, from external suggestion as to the
lines along which thought may travel, and the unfettered will may be expressed.

It is, doubtless, difficult in many cases to ascribe to
a particular story the part played in its evolution by
domestic influences on the child. Still, the story will
generally carry with it sufficient evidence to justify the
conclusion as to the independent action of the child's
mind.

The illustrations could be indefinitely multiplied, but
these are sufficiently numerous for the purpose. "As
a child thinketh in his heart, so is he." But the importance of his thinking will be greater or less in the
formation of opinion as to what a child essentially is,
when we are able to state how much the thought is
the child's, and how far the thought has been put into
its head by another.

From the instances adduced, there is overwhelming
evidence in favour of the divinity of the child's origin ;

and this is the main conclusion it is sought to establish in these pages.

The study of childhood is not less worthy than the investigation of the beginnings of things by the geologist, or the chemist, or the natural philosopher.

CHAPTER III.

THE SEAMY SIDE OF CHILD-NATURE.

To affirm, without qualification, that a child comes into the world complete and perfect would be as absurd as it is untrue. It begins its existence as a bundle of potentialities. It is full of the most tender susceptibilities. It is a delicately strung musical instrument. A sympathetic touch will elicit the sweetest tones; an ignorant rough-handed person will evoke all manner of discordant noises.

In the preceding chapter the life is traced in its unfolding and during its most early stages, mainly under loving and wise conditions, and, as a rule, brightest anticipations have been fulfilled. The child has grown, and its growth has been watched with satisfaction and delight by those most solicitous for its welfare.

But the proper treatment of the infant must be directed by a just appreciation of its necessities and its claims, and these can only be decided upon after a careful study of the nature of the child. But who is sufficient for these things?

It is no exaggeration to say that a young mother or a nurse-girl, into whose hands the babe first comes,

will more frequently than not, be ignorant of its constitution, and quite unprepared for the duties of its
education, whether physical, mental or moral. The
child, as a consequence of neglect or mistaken kindness, is troublesome, disagreeable, crying, passionate.
It soon acquires a bad character, and if its parents be
theological, the little one is set down as a remarkable
victim of the fall of Adam, though the real cause of the
mischief is more likely to be the fall of the baby
through the heedlessness of the nurse.

Accident, blunder, bad temper, over-indulgence in the
nurse, will generally be at the bottom of the manifestation of evil in the babe, and neither Adam nor his
latest descendent can fairly be held responsible for
what we call the seamy side of childhood.

It must not be forgotten that heredity, through the
wickedness of its ancestors, may have entailed in the
poor infant constitutional evils that no training will be
able to eradicate; but the fact ought to excite more
tender pity and enlist the fuller sympathy.

A new-born babe may be said to be morally perfect
though its perfection is purely negative. As yet it
knows neither good nor evil. It is, as yet, unmoral,
simple; and its simplicity as regards what is evil, is
that which the Apostle Paul desired for his disciples.

Fostered by a wise and tender nurse, the infant's
sensitive nature, like a small fragile craft launched
upon the stream of time, will be screened from the
blasts of cutting winds, sheltered from the collisions

to which it is exposed, and kept out of the currents which threaten to make it an early wreck.

On the other hand, supposing the babe to fall into the hands of an unsympathetic nurse whose handling is provocative of discomfort and whose mistakes arouse reflex feelings against the injury done ; an Augustinian theorist would be at once satisfied that such a specimen offers an infantile demonstration of the doctrine of Adamic corruption.

May we not take a more generous, nay, a more just view of the little stranger, and find out some more reasonable, more hopeful, and more God-like explanation of the evils which sooner or later present themselves for observation in the experience and behaviour of the precious infant ?

Take, for instance, the manifestation of " anger." " A worm will turn when it is trodden upon," and a baby suffering pain, generally by accident in manipulating the tender little thing—it may be a pin accidentally stuck into its body—will betray the suffering in response to the violent stimulus.

In the early part of its existence, as James Hinton says, its actions have no moral value ; the child is neither moral nor immoral but *unmoral.*

Presently, with a certain measure of experience, it learns that crying brings help and deliverance. A friendly hand puts matters right. A scream in an infant is often a kindly warning to a mother that a wrong has been done or a duty neglected.

With advancing intelligence it learns the value of tears as a means of getting what it wants; or, as a weapon of offence, the tears stand as the symbol of dislike, or of revenge for being deprived of a toy without seeing any reason why it should be treated so badly.

Our primitive ancestors, characterised by impulsiveness and often by extreme irascibility, may fairly be debited with some of this evil tendency; and this tendency, supplemented by the ignorant, mischievous, and often cruel treatment of parents, will hardly fail to develop a monstrous character.

Caprice in a little creature of eleven months manifested itself in a violent temper, because she vainly tried to seize her grandfather's nose.

Perez placed this passion among the class of animal sentiments.

Jealousy, again, is more or less common among all animals. A gentleman of the writer's acquaintance, cannot make any demonstration of affection to his wife but the collie immediately gets excited with jealousy; and ceases his barking and is at peace, as soon as some attention is shown to him. Who has not seen a jealous child making itself wretched at its parents' mutual caresses?

A child sometimes covets a thing not for the sake of enjoying it, but because it does not like to see another possessing it.

Cruelty.

What is called cruelty is generally the result of the unreasoning manner in which a child will conduct its investigations of the phenomena which come under its notice. A child is attracted by a fly on the window pane. The movements of the fly stimulate the attempts to take possession of the poor insect. The child has no intention of harming the fly; he only wants to examine the object to which his attention is drawn. Very likely the fly gets damaged ; and if the pursuit of knowledge makes the child a vivisectionist, and the fly loses a wing or a leg, it is not necessarily the consequence of cruelty in the child, but merely an unfortunate incident in the pursuit of knowledge.

Resentment.

A child takes offence, anger is aroused, and desire for retaliation is excited. But like the feelings of children, pleasurable or painful, the passion is not very deep; and it is very rare for a child to cherish resentful thoughts.

The reconciler.

The following true story confirms the view proposed, that the evil thoughts of a little child are more akin to

the ruffling of the surface of the lake, than the lashing
into fury of the raging sea.

Mrs. G. was out one day when she came upon a
group of children. At the moment, a man was re-
proving a little boy of four or five, for kicking his
sister. He passed on and now my friend took the
case in hand, and urged the offender to kiss his sister
and be good. He flushed with anger, and was
obstinate. Mrs. G. then said to the little girl :—" You
kiss him, then." This she did at once, and the little
fellow was conquered ; he flung his arms round her
neck, and the reconciliation was complete. A penny
for some sweets crowned the new-found happiness.

Quarrelsome children.

Richard and Jane are always quarrelling (ages only
three and four). One day the waves of contention ran
high—each was claiming the possession of the moon !

An old man, not far from eighty, tells me that the
most vivid recollection of his own childhood is that at
three his passion was aroused, and he lay upon a form,
striking out and daring anybody to come near him.

Dissimulation.

Training is necessary to make a child a dissembler.
A fifth of November mask over its face looks tempting,
but it is not long before it feels hot and uncomfortable,
and the child cannot tolerate the stifling thing that

comes between it and the fresh air of heaven. Disguises are for grown-up people who can't walk straight.

Comparing notes with the young Prince of Asturias, afterwards King of Spain, the French Prince Imperial one day asked him what lesson he found it hardest to learn. "It is," said the then future King of Spain dismally, "not to laugh when I am amused at the theatre."

"They let me laugh as much as I like," said the Prince Imperial; "but what I don't like is to be obliged to smile and look pleasant to men whom I know are my father's enemies."

He was specially alluding to Count Bismarck, who had come on a visit to Napoleon III. at Plombieres, and had been received with a cordiality which the boy knew to be more apparent than real.

Force of example.

A little girl only fifteen months old had already begun to imitate her father's frown and irritable ways and angry voice ; and very soon after she learnt to use expressions of anger and impatience. When three years old, this same little girl gravely said to a visitor at the house, with whom she had begun to argue quite in her father's style:—"Do be quiet, will you, you never let me finish my sentences."

Lying.

Lying has its root in distrust. Trust is the normal state of a child's nature. But its suspicion is soon aroused by a harsh word or a frown, confidence is gone, fear is excited, a sense of wrong somewhere is engendered. The child is right in *trying to please*, but the thing to *please* is said instead of the thing which is true in the hope of averting some evil.

Care should always be taken to ascertain whether a little child is conscious of what a lie means. At two years of age Harry told a lie and was corrected by his mother. He looked at her through his tears and said, "What is a lie, a thing you put in your pocket?" An explanation sufficed and he never again swerved from the truth.

Envy and pride.

Envy springs out of a sense of one's own supposed inferiority to another's real or imagined superiority. Pride results from one's own imagined superiority to another's fancied inferiority. If pride fail of the recognition it claims, it becomes a cause of irritation to its possessor.

John Ruskin maintains that pride is at the bottom of most of the miserable mistakes that are made.

The seeds of pride are very early sown in a child's heart. Fond and foolish mothers are among the most frequent and successful sowers. They put the seeds into fine clothes. They drop them into the ears of their children while they talk to their friends of the pretty faces and charming ways of their little ones. Instead of checking they will sometimes applaud the sauciness and the haughtiness, which, before all things, they ought to be concerned to eradicate or uproot.

Cunning.

A little girl, of three years, was young enough to be put to sleep every afternoon. One day she found that her mother was going out in the afternoon. She objected, and begged her mother not to go. But her appeal could not be listened to, and nurse took her to her bedroom and put her down to sleep in her bed. The nurse left the room and then the little thing got out of bed, found her mother's boots and concealed them. Time was lost in hunting for the missing boots : the search was unsuccessful. The mother could not go out. When the child woke from her sleep she was discovered with one boot under each arm.

Praying children.

What? it will be asked, are not children to pray? The reader will frame his answer to the question, when he has read the following.

A little boy reminded God on one occasion that his

petition had "not been attended to," and requested
that it might not be forgotten in future.

The same child had been offended by his governess.
His mother saw him burying a piece of paper on this
occasion in the garden. When she was able, unseen
by the child, to dig up the paper, she discovered that
it was a request to the devil to take the governess
below.

We talk of virgin soil, and of its prolific character.
This is the soul of a little child. The moral is: Take
heed what you sow.

The environment of the child should be healthy and
suitable to its years. Let the sowing be "wind," and
its friends will reap "the whirlwind;" for as we sow,
we reap.

Disappointing lives come of *neglect*, injudicious training, and often of the most fearful errors in the
teacher.

Total depravity; or fading light. Which?

Lord Shaftesbury relates the story of one of the waifs
and strays of London, who was in the habit of sleeping
at night within a large iron roller in the Regent's Park.
The boy found another lad who had not where to lay
his head, and at his invitation the 'neighbour' shared
his iron bedstead with him.

"During his perambulations of the slums of London
in 1846, by his ragged school investigations, &c., Lord

Ashley made himself thoroughly acquainted with the haunts and habits of the young thieves of the metropolis."

"A large proportion do not recognize the distinctive rights of *meum* and *tuum*. Property appears to them to be only the aggregate of plunder. They hold that everything that is possessed is common stock : that he who gets most is the cleverest fellow, and that everyone has a right to abstract from that stock what he can by his own ingenuity. With them there is no sense of shame, nor is imprisonment received as a disgrace."*

Lord Shaftesbury recorded this, having received it from the lips of a City missionary, a kind and worthy man who had endeared himself to the whole of a wretched district, and especially to the younger population.

"One evening having put on a new coat, he went, about dusk, through a remote street, and was instantly marked as a quarry by one of these rapacious vagabonds. The urchin did not know him in his new attire,—therefore without hesitation relieved his pockets of their contents. The missionary did not discover his loss, nor did the boy his victim, until in his flight he had reached the end of the street. He then looked round and recognized in the distance his old friend and teacher. *He ran back to him, breathless.* "Hullo," said

* Edwin Hodder's *Life and Works of Lord Shaftesbury.* Vol. ii., p. 263

he, "is it you Mr. ———? I didn't know you in
your new coat; here's your handkerchief for you!"*

The spoiled child.

In a subsequent chapter we have attempted to present the child, welcomed by Jesus Christ, as an ideal
of the kingdom of Heaven, but we may here ask the
question :—What is a spoiled child?

The spoiled child is a child that nobody likes. His
presence in a home makes that home a misery; and
he must be an exceptionally hopeful person who will
predict for that child a career of happiness and pros-
perity.

He is not, unfortunately, so uncommon as to render
it necessary to portray his character, and it would be
deemed superfluous were we to attempt to describe the
means of *spoliation.*

One is struck at the outset with the term "*spoiled.*"
To spoil is (literally) to strip off, to plunder. And we
cannot help remarking the essential identity of the
nature of the "spoiling," whether we observe it in the
occurrence which took place on the eve of the departure of the Israelites from Egypt, when "they
spoiled the Egyptians"; or whether we trace it in a
destructive child who spoils his toy; or whether it is
forced upon our attention in an indulgent parent who
spoils his child.

* *Ibid.,* p. 264.

The spoiling in each case is identical. That is, there is a stripping, or deprivation, of some valuable property which belonged to the object spoiled. The spoiled Egyptians were deprived of their material treasures. The spoiled toy is deprived of its essential properties as a plaything. And the spoiled child is deprived or suffers the loss of those precious qualities which make childhood so sweet and attractive.

What makes the spoiled child of the home so sad and so serious a matter is, that the home of that child is usually responsible for the domestic trouble. The spoliation is effected, not by outsiders, but by relatives, and more frequently than not, by an ignorant indulgent father or mother.

Still, the spoiled child is the exception rather than the rule. At least we have found it so, whether we have studied childhood in the homes of comfort and ease, or in the more humble families of poverty and privation.

We have watched children in the Sunday school. Take the infant class. Discouragement has come at the very outset of our work, for here and there has turned up a spoiled child of the home. The boy chafes at the restraint of school rules, and finds it a great bore to have to learn anything at all; the girl's attention is diverted by her bright ribbon, or flower-decked hat, from any serious attempt to forget herself and her petted prettiness, while both boy and girl have been supplied with light refreshments in the shape of "sweets." But, happily, these are the exceptions, not the rule. The little ones, as yet, have Heaven on their side; and though the world is all *before* them, it is not in them ; and almost any one of them might be taken by the great Teacher, at random, and his beautiful lesson would not suffer from a nineteenth century text. For we doubt not he would still say to the disciples—and are we not all His disciples?—"Except ye be converted and become as this little child . . . . "

Now, what the parent is to the home, that the teacher is to the Sunday school class. And the Sunday scholar may become a spoiled child even when the teacher, with the utmost conscientiousness and affectionate interestedness, is loading the child with *his* good things. Verily, paradoxical as it may appear, the spoiling of the home and the spoiling of the school, are both the result, mainly, of overloading the child.

The injudicious gifts of the home are the very means by which the child suffers loss of his most precious endowments; and the overloading by the teacher of the innocent child effects a similar result.

In either case, the child is being spoiled by receiving too much; or in other words is not getting truly at all, but is being stripped of his rightful property. "I am rich and increased in goods" is simply the utterance of the spoiled child "writ large."

But *how* are little children spoiled in the Sunday school ?

Our answer to the question will be better understood by first recognizing the fact that a little child
is supposed to be most suitably welcomed to the
school with a feeling in the mind of the teacher akin
to *pity*—" poor little thing ! "

" Well," says an impatient reader, " weakness is a
prominent feature in a little child, and surely our pity
is not thrown away here."

Think, my friend, whether your pity, though natural,
for it is closely allied to sympathy, is the feeling that
should have the fullest and deepest current in your
heart, when you receive " one such little one." Do
you not remember that the Master said :—" He that
receiveth one such little one receiveth me ?" Did John
pity " the lamb of God," when he drew the attention of
his disciples to the gentle Jesus ? (John i. 36). How
often, if you have been a careful observer of God's
ways in history, have you noticed that He has *chosen*
the weak things of the world to confound the mighty.
Nay, from our worldly estimate of Power, how weak
is the Almighty! Even His high purposes seem to be
sown in weakness, but only that they may be raised in
power.

How remarkable is the power of a little child to
arrest attention, to excite sympathy, to provoke to
love! How spontaneous, disinterested, and ungrudg-
ing the help we proffer ; how irresistible its un-
conscious demands ! And yet this word—*irresistible*—
as appropriate as any we can think of, suggests not

merely power but omnipotence. How often, when others have vainly sought to move you from your purpose, and you have triumphantly opposed the temptation to relinquish your occupation, have you given in to the silent but eloquent appeal of a little pair of eyes. All else might be successfully withstood, but "the child has won the day."

Our pity, then, is somewhat superfluous, but as this is not often mischievous in its effect in the Sunday school, we will pass on to the consideration of more serious and pernicious means of spoliation. And we notice—

The superinduction on the natural spirituality of the child of an artificial religiousness.

"Seeming to be religious," summed up the character of some members of the early Christian church ; and, without being uncharitable or censorious, it must be admitted that it describes the Christianity of many in the present day.

Think of the child as a plant. To secure a healthy plant, the soil must be good ; sunshine and rain are essential ; fresh air and suitable temperature must be obtained. A plant may be robbed of its vigour, its growth may be stopped, and decay will be hastened by withdrawing it from its natural requirements. The child may be robbed of its beauty, its power of development, in the same way. Withdraw it from Divine resources, and give it artificial light, heat, atmosphere— and it will be spoiled.

Thus by inducing an artificial and superficial religiousness, the qualities which Jesus commended in the child are being weakened, repressed or destroyed.

There must, doubtless, be regulations of time for lessons and worship, but these should interfere as little as possible with the life and freshness of the individual pupils.

A still more serious means of spoliation, whether in the home or in the school class, is the neglect of the spiritual by the substitution of the cultivation of the intellectual.

The stimulus given to secular learning of late years has been extraordinary. It is largely due to competition. Education has not been primarily the object, but the *successful passing of "Exams."*—The method—cramming. The end of the tutor may be attained; but the pupil, instead of being prepared by educational processes for the affairs of life, is often little else than *pâté de foie gras.*

So with the education of the soul. Its faculties may lie dormant, while the memory is being stored with the scientific or doctrinal system of Theology of the schools. Instead of bread—a stone.

More than this. Whole books of the Bible may be committed to memory while the soul of the child is being starved.

The soul is not a tank for storing the water of life, but an organism whose vigour and growth must be constantly nourished by the living water.

Theology may map out to the mind the goodly land with faithful and minute detail. It may trace its rivers, describe its mountains, its cities, its rich pastures, its mineral wealth, its natural products; but a life-long study of the map will never put one in possession of the goodly land. The journey must be begun. The land must be entered. The grapes must be gathered. The fields must be cultivated. And for all this, the energies of the man must be put forth, and in their unfolding the strength will be increased.

The end of spiritual education, then, is not a cramming of the mind with knowledge, but a development of spiritual faculty in discernment, in holy resolve, in purity of living, and in wise and loving action.

One of the first attempts in the elementary education of a baby is to get it to stand upon its feet, and to encourage it to run alone. Here we have the great function of the true spiritual teacher clearly expressed. He must help the child to *stand* and to *walk*. You may *spoil* the child by artificial support and everlasting perambulator.

Means of spoliation.

There are many ways in which a child may be spoiled. Unintentionally and ignorantly the spoiling of a child goes on; and there is often a rude awakening, when the eyes of the *spoiler* are opened.

Keeping before our mind the essential elements of

the spiritual nature of the child we notice its *un-conscious gentleness and humility*. This results from a sense of its dependence on another, its feeble resources of mind and body, and the very narrow limits of its experience; and is not this humility one of the great charms of a little child?

The self-consciousness of a little child is quickly aroused; and with consciousness of self the spoiling has begun. The humility of the child is endangered.

Take, for instance, the recitation of poetry before company or in public, after forcing the little brain to commit it to memory; the subjects being most frequently unsuited to the capacity and sphere of the child, and even unintelligible.

That shrewd and sympathetic observer, Dr. Johnson, understood this. He was exceedingly disposed to indulge children, and ceremoniously careful not to offend them. He was, however, full of indignation against such parents as delight to bring their young ones too early into the talking world, and was known to give a good deal of pain by refusing to hear the verses that a child could recite. This was the case on one occasion when a lady brought her two children to him. Gray's *Elegy* might become comic in the mouths of little children; but Johnson would not have Gray any more than the children spoiled. When he was told the children would recite a verse alternately, he said;— "No, let them both recite at once, and then the noise will be sooner over."

Why fasten mechanically exotic flowers, however lovely, on the slight stems of a young and tender plant ?

The stimulus of injudicious and often exaggerated praise of a child brought forward to perform some clever feat, endangers humility by encouraging pride.

Still more ignoble the ambition of a parent to enhance the natural charms of childhood by dressing it in clothes in which pride again is often fostered. Who would paint the lily? " Be clothed with humility."

Still more serious is the despoiling a child of its *faith.* How a child's trust wins the heart ! And yet an unsuspecting child may suffer a strange revulsion of feeling, an astonishment of dismay, when for the first time it is aroused from its sweet restfulness of soul by a deceptive word or action. A new and baneful experience this, which may lead to the most disastrous consequences in character and life.

A brutal soldier may with a firebrand destroy the most gorgeous temple; but this is a trifle compared with the destruction of the faith of a little child. It were better for the offender to be cast, with a millstone round his neck, into the midst of the sea.

Rob a child of his faith—an element of his true nature—and he is spoiled indeed.

Not less sad and disastrous is the assault on a child's heart. This is the citadel of the affections. Yet it may be chilled by a sinister glance; shocked by a hasty word ; broken by an unjust or harsh judgment.

Better err a thousand times on the side of over-appreciation, or even of praise, than wound the tender blind affection of a generous little soul.

In a little child it is quite possible for the wine of love to turn to the vinegar of hate. Nor would the love be so chargeable with weakness or fickleness, as the unjust, unkind and capricious conduct of a parent who is really responsible for the change. The hate may be truer to the genuineness of the heart's best affection, than a love weak and indefinite, which can live unperturbed amid the discouragement inflicted by those who should encourage and strengthen it.

Parental love may be profusely demonstrative and lavish in its gifts, but it may altogether fail of its best fruits. Its capriciousness may wound the heart ; its unwise gifts may foster selfishness. And here one detects the busy hand of spoliation.

The heart does not live on toys and luxuries, but in the admired and trusted affection of the parent.

In this chapter facts have been adduced which reveal the child in the least favourable light. Apart from any preconceived theory and approaching the consideration of childhood in the spirit of honest inquiry, what would be the fair conclusion suggested ? It ought never to be forgotten that an infant is endowed with faculties which from the earliest period are more sensitive to impressions, more delicately responsive to the touch, than at any subsequent stages of its existence.

Now when we speak of the seamy side of childhood,

we may be thinking of *essential attributes* as necessarily including a bias to evil, or a radically evil or sinful nature.   This is not the sense in which we are using the words.

Hereditary taints of evil may reveal themselves in some little individual specimen of humanity, just as hereditary mental and moral excellencies may be early manifested in another specimen.   But each of these may be special varieties, whilst the essential attributes of the type are not to be overlooked.

But beyond and apart from what must be conceded to the modifying power of heredity, the seamy side of childhood will be found to be largely due to evil training, to the persisting and corrupting influence of bad example and to the unholy thoughts of the heart and the wicked practices of the hands.

There can be nothing to be astonished at in a child who has been allowed to develop under conditions which are favourable only to that which is evil; and in reviewing the instances of a naughty childhood we often marvel at the intuitions of a love, and a purity, and a generosity, which sometimes discover themselves in a young life that seems to be practically lost.

Such cases suggest rather an inextinguishable, or at least a fading light, before the dark clouds of vice into which the young life is forced, than a being who brings with it from its birth a nature which can only be developed along the lines of the earthly, sensual and devilish.   The seamy side of the child is not, therefore, essential to the child-nature but is due to the deplorable conditions under which the child is developed; and if instances are carefully studied the evil may be easily traced to the viciousness of the atmosphere which the child has been unable to escape.

Evolution and heredity.

" The most beautiful witness to the evolution of man is the mind of a little child," says Henry Drummond; " evolution, after all, is the study of the nursery."

Just as the dissecting room affords the most ample opportunity for acquiring a knowledge of the anatomy of the human body, the nursery supplies the largest facilities for the collection of facts which illustrate the functions and development of the human mind.

In the child we have before us a clue to the history of mankind from the most primitive times. The first year of a child's life may represent the full-grown prehistoric man. The gradual development of the infant mind, year by year, supplies an epitome of the growth of the race. This is no mere conjecture. There are still races existing on the earth's surface whose mental status and attainments are about on a level with those of a baby. It cannot be said that the progress of these races has been arrested, for it has scarcely yet begun. The field of observation includes the lowest type of primeval men and all the inter-

H

mediate stages of ancient and modern civilization, up to the highest style of spiritual development that man has reached under the influence of the purest religion in the present day. The whole process is shadowed forth in a porcelain factory, where you behold at one inspection the china clay and the various processes through which it passes in the manufacture to the finished vase.

But more than this. Not only can the earliest stages of mental evolution be studied in living specimens on the face of the earth ; not only is the nursery a microcosm in which the various phases of mental evolution are traceable, but according to Romanes, the nursery also discloses the *order* in which the faculties of the mind are developed.

In Romanes' books on *Animal Intelligence* and on *Mental Evolution in Animals*, he gives us the results of his observations on animals. Taking the emotions, as one set of phenomena, to which he devoted special attention, with the view of detecting the order of their development in various stages of animal life, he came to the following conclusions :—

Fear.	Sympathy.	Benevolence.
Surprise.	Emulation.	Revenge.
Affection.	Pride.	Rage.
Pugnacity.	Resentment.	Shame.
Curiosity.	Emotion of the beautiful.	Regret.
Jealousy.	Grief.	Deceit.
Anger.	Hate.	Emotion of the
Play.	Cruelty.	ludicrous.

Let parents observe their offspring with regard not only to the fact of the existence of these feelings but with reference to their earliest manifestations, and they may find confirmation of the conclusions at which Romanes arrived.

It is not necessary to the scope of this Essay to follow Romanes through his argument, though it is full of deep interest.

There is yet another doctrine of more immediate importance as bearing on the nature of the child, and that is the doctrine of heredity.

Evolution and heredity are not by any means opposed to one another. In connection with evolution we are supplied with the general principles of reproduction. By heredity we learn the differentiation which results from special influences, such as education, occupation, disease, &c.

Evolution illustrates the progress of the species. Heredity explains the specific variations of type. Heredity is an universally admitted principle, which accounts for family and national idiosyncrasies.

Orthodox theology has fastened itself on the law of heredity greatly to the disparagement of the little child, and to the discouragement of those who have the charge of its training.

Evolution encourages hope as it postulates man's gradual ascent from a lower to a higher range of being, and anticipates the ultimate triumph of the spirit over the flesh.

The theology which condemns (we cannot say welcomes) a little stranger into our home as the miserable outcome of an awful catastrophe, called " the Fall," logically though cruelly fastens upon the race the radical taint of depravity, and would clothe us in the garments of mourning and despair.

Heredity explains the transmitted virtuous tendencies of the good, no less than the transmitted vicious tendencies of the bad. But evolution, holding on its upward way, is ever on the side of hope and improvement.

The pessimist would not admire this rose-coloured picture of development, and he would, doubtless, adduce facts less favourable to the progressive than to the retrogressive theory. What has he to say? He would point to the birds or fishes, whose forms have undergone modification by altered conditions; whose sight has been lost by withdrawal from light; and other instances of disused faculty resulting in its ultimate extinction. Much might be brought forward of the effect of disused or of unused faculties, of mind as well as of body. The process is illustrated by familiar examples, physical, mental and moral, under the modifying influence of circumstances. Weismann points out many causes and conditions of retrogressive development in nature; but allowing for these remarkable instances of retrogression, the outcome of evolution is generally favourable to progress and improvements, and opposed to degeneration.

Three distinct stages are noticeable facts in the progress from inorganic matter and motion up to the highest and most complex existence—man. 1. The change from inorganic to organic matter. 2. The further development from organic matter to sentient consciousness; constituting the distinction between the vegetable and animal kingdoms. 3. The existence in man of a number of his noblest faculties, and most remarkable characteristics, pointing to a universe of Spirit, to which the world of matter is altogether subordinate.

The environment of a child explains and illustrates the laws of its development. It is particularly interesting to observe the order in which the evolution from the lower, that is the sensuous, to the higher intellectual faculties takes place. This may be considered in the following order: 1. The musical. 2. The artistic. 3. The metaphysical or abstract. 4. The mathematical; and as some add, 5. Wit and humour.

Of the higher faculties, we put musical impressions and expressions earliest, because we perceive that the senses have a part to play in the perception and development of musical ideas. The consciousness of sound, with elevation and depression of pitch in its sequence of tones, and early acquirement of acquaintance with that succession and relation of notes which form a tune and rhythm.

So with regard to the artistic faculty. The intelligence readily combines its subjective idea with the report of the sense of sight, and pictures become a means of "the higher education."

It has often been noticed how inadequate are the powers of the untutored savage to manage the simplest mathematical process—numeration—and how quickly he finds himself out of his depth!

Wit and humour are the outcome of an appreciation of plain facts, touched by poetic imagination, or at least by a sense of fitness of harmony or contrast of ideas, giving rise to more or less ludicrous observations.

The spiritual, the supreme part of man's nature, as it is almost undefinable, is hardly to be reckoned as one of the series of mental phenomena, more than it is to be regarded as a sensuous or emotional state. It is cognizable through the emotions, as well as through the intellect, it melts in tears, or it may harden in mental states. At first it is a mere possibility, but at a very early period it will develop into activity by a breath of the Divine Spirit. Fuller discussion of this is reserved for a future chapter.

CHAPTER IV.

THE CHILD OF HEATHENDOM.

HAVING at some length discussed the characteristics of childhood in numerous instances, to which an observant reader might add to almost any extent, it will be worth while to notice the place the child has occupied in some of the ancient civilizations, and also to observe the influence of the civilization and religions of various countries upon children.

It might be expected that an advanced civilization would be favourable to the well-being of the child, and that the children of barbarous peoples would be placed at a great disadvantage, but it is not always so, as will be seen further on.

Neither is religion any guarantee of the child's protection and happiness. With some "the sacred rites of religion" have included the sacrifice of innocent children, who have had a back-handed compliment paid to them by those who have offered "the fruit of the body for the sin of the soul."

And again, the heathen have often put to shame, in their care of children, the boasted superiority of Christian nations.

THE CHILDREN OF EGYPT.

Following Wilkinson,* who quotes from Plato, we learn that "in the education of youth they were particularly strict; and 'they knew,' says Plato, 'that children ought to be early accustomed to such gestures, looks, and motions as are decent and proper, and not be suffered to either hear or learn any verses and songs, than those which are calculated to inspire them with virtue; and they consequently took care that every dance and ode introduced at their feasts or sacrifices should be subject to certain regulations.' They particularly inculcated respect for old age; and the fact of this being required even towards strangers, argues a great regard for the person of a parent; for we are informed that, like the Israelites and the Lacedæmonians, they required every young man to give place to his superiors in years, and even if seated to rise on their approach.

"Nor were these honours limited to their life-time: the memory of parents and ancestors was revered through succeeding generations: their tombs were maintained with the greatest respect; liturgies were performed by the children, or by priests at their expense."

If WOMEN *are respected we may be pretty sure that* CHILDREN *will be well treated and trained.*

* *Ancient Egyptians*, vol. ii., 1854.

"In primitive ages the duties of women were very different from those of later and more civilised periods, and varied of course according to the habits of each people. Among pastoral tribes they drew water, kept the sheep, and superintended the herds as well as the flocks. As with the Arabs of the present day, they prepared both the furniture and the woollen stuffs of which the tents themselves were made, ground the corn, and performed other menial offices. They were also engaged, as in ancient Greece, in weaving, spinning, needlework, embroidery, and other sedentary occupations within doors. The Egyptian ladies in like manner employed much of their time with the needle ; and the sculptures represent many females weaving and using the spindle. But they were not kept in the same secluded manner as those of ancient Greece, who, besides being confined to certain apartments in the house most remote from the hall of entrance, and generally in the uppermost part of the building, were not even allowed to go out of doors without a veil, as in many Oriental countries of the present day. The Egyptians treated their women very differently, as the accounts of ancient authors and the sculptures sufficiently prove. At some of the public festivals women were expected to attend—not alone, like the Moslem women at a mosque, but in company with their husbands or relations."*

Such was the position to which woman had attained

* *Ibid.*, vol. ii., p. 224.

in Egypt, and the honour in which she was held, that she sometimes became the supreme ruler.

We get a glimpse of regard for childhood among the Egyptians in the beautiful story of Pharaoh's daughter, in connection with the finding of Moses. " Take this child and nurse it for me," reveals the love of the mother and the leadership of the princess.

ANCIENT GREECE.

We cannot give a better idea of the high appreciation of childhood by the best minds of Greece than by quoting Plato as translated by the late Professor Jowett.*

" Plato's views of education are in several respects remarkable. Like the rest of the Republic, they are partly Greek and partly ideal, beginning with the ordinary curriculum of the Greek youth, and extending to after life. *Plato* is the *first* writer who distinctly expresses the thought that *education is to comprehend the whole of life,* and to be a preparation for another in which education is to begin again. This is the continuous thread which runs through the whole of the Republic, and which more than any other of his ideas admits of an application to modern life."†

" *His conception of education is represented, not like*

* *Dialogues of Plato translated into English. The Republic,* vol. ii., 1871.

† *Introduction,* p. 152.

many modern views, under the image of filling a vessel, but of turning the eye of the soul towards the light."*

" The principles on which religion is to be based are two only; first, that God is true; secondly, that He is good. Modern and Christian writers have fallen short of these; they can hardly be said to have got beyond them."†

" But the honourable mind which is to form a healthy judgment ought rather to have had no experience or contamination of evil habits when young. And this is the reason why in youth good men often appear to be simple, and are easily practised upon by the evil, because they have no samples of evil in their own souls."‡

The education of the children is under discussion :—

" You know that the beginning is the chiefest part of any work, especially in a young and tender thing; for that is the time at which the character is formed and most readily receives the desired impression.

" Quite true.

" And shall we just carelessly allow children to hear any casual tales which may be framed by casual persons, and to receive into their minds notions which are the very opposite of those which are to be held by them when they are grown up ?

" We cannot allow that.

" Then the first thing will be to have a censorship of the writers of fiction, and let the censors receive any

* *Ibid.*, p. 153.   † *Ibid.*, p. 154.   ‡ *Ibid.*, p. 236.

tale of fiction which is good, and reject the bad; and we will allow the mothers and nurses to tell their children the authorized ones only. . . . . . At the same time most of those which are now in use will have to be discarded. . . . .

"But which are the stories that you mean, he said, and what fault do you find with them?

"A fault which is most serious, I said, the fault of telling a lie, and a bad *lie*."*

And then he goes on to discuss the stories which should be kept from children, the *cruelties* of the gods, the misrepresentation of the state of the dead, as one to shrink from.

"And we must beg Homer and other poets not to be angry if we strike out these and similar passages, not because they are unpoetical, or unattractive to the popular ear, but because the greater charm of them as poetry, the less are they meet for the ears of boys and men, who are to be sons of freedom and are to fear slavery more than death.

"Also we shall have to reject all the terrible and appalling names which describe the world below—Cocytus and Styx, ghosts under the earth, and sapless shades, and any other words of the same type, the very mention of which causes a shudder to pass through the inmost soul of him who hears them. I do not say that these tales may not have a use of some kind, but there is a danger that *the nerves of our guardians may become affected by them.*"†

* *Ibid.*, Book II., p. 201. † *Ibid.*, Book III., p. 210.

The following is mainly from Plato :—*

" The first year is the beginning of the whole life to everyone; which ought to be written in the temples of their fathers, as the beginning of life, both to a boy and girl."

In discussing the treatment of the child, even in embryo, and its physical treatment after birth, the following occurs :—

" All bodies are benefited by shakings and motion, when moved without weariness, of all that are moved by themselves, or by swings, or carried on the sea, or on horseback, or borne along in any manner soever by other bodies, and through these getting the mastery over food and drink, *they are able to impart to us health, and beauty, and the rest of strength.*"†

" Since then such is the case, what shall we say that we ought to do after this ?   Are you willing for us to say with a laugh, that we are laying down laws for the pregnant woman to walk about, and to *mould the infant as a thing of wax, while it is yet flexible,* and to put it in swathing clothes until it is two years old ; and that we are moreover compelling the nurses by legal fines to carry the children either into the fields, or to the temples, or their acquaintance, until they are sufficiently able to stand alone ; and then that they should be careful, lest by the limbs becoming distorted, while forcibly resting on them, being still young, to undergo

* *The Laws,* translated by Burges.. Book VI., Chap. xxiii., p. 248.
† Book VII., p. 251.

the additional labour of carrying the infant, until it had completed its third year; and that the nurses ought to be as strong as possible; and, in addition, that unless these things take place to each child, we are to enact a fine upon those who do not so act? or is this far from being the case? For that, which has just now been mentioned, would happen to us without stint.

"*Clin.* What is that?

"*Athen.* To pay the debt of abundant laughter, through the womanlike and servile manners of the nurses being unwilling to obey us."*

"*Athen.* Let us then receive this as an element with respect to both the circumstances, (the body and soul,) of the very young, that the nursing and motion, taking place as much as possible all the night and day, are profitable to all, and not the least to the youngest; so that, if it were possible, they may live as if always sailing on the sea. But now, (since this is impossible), it is requisite to act as near as possible to this with respect to the newly born nurslings of children. . . . . . . When mothers are desirous to put to sleep their children, who sleep with difficulty, they do not bring them to a state of quietness, but, on the contrary, of *motion*, by shaking them ever in their arms; nor yet that of *silence*, but that of singing to them; and they artlessly soothe their children, as it were, by the sound of a pipe, and, as the remedies of

* *Ibid.*, Book VII., Chap. ii., p. 252.

the mad Bacchants are employed, by making use, at the same time, of the movements in music and the dance.

" *Clin.* What then, O guest, is especially the cause of this ?

" *Athen.* It is not very difficult to know.

" *Clin.* How so ?

" *Athen.* Both these passions result from fear ; and there are certain terrors through a depraved habit of soul. When therefore any one brings from without an agitation to passions of this kind, that which is from without overcomes the dreadful and insane motion within ; and after overcoming, it seems to have produced a calm in the soul, and a quietness in the leaping, which had been troublesome as regards the heart of each; (and) thus, (what is) altogether agreeable, it causes some to obtain by lot* sleep; but others, who are awake, and dancing and soothed by the pipe under the influence of the divinities, (or as we say, ' by the blessing of God '), to whom each may be supplicating and sacrificing, it causes to possess habits of sound sense in the place of a maddened state. Now this, to speak in brief, has in this way a certain probable reason."†

After alluding to timidity and fortitude, moroseness and courage :—

" *Athen.* In what manner then is to be implanted which of these we may wish in the newly born ? We

* The text is somewhat confused, Burges says.
† *Ibid.*, p. 254.

must endeavour to state how and to what extent a person may have an easy road in these matters.

" *Clin.* How not ?

" *Athen. I will mention then the fixed opinion with us, that luxury renders the manners of youth morose and irascible, and vehemently agitated by things of a trifling nature ;* but that an excessive and rustic servitude causes them to be contrary to this, abject and illiberal, and man-haters, and unfitting associates.

" *Clin.* But how will the whole state be able to bring up those, who have as yet no perception of language, and are unable to have any taste for the rest of instruction ?

" *Athen.* Somehow in this way. Every animal, as soon as it is born, is wont to utter some sound with a loud cry, and not the least the human species ; and more than the rest of animals it is affected in addition to its crying with the shedding of tears.

" *Clin.* Entirely so.

" *Athen.* Now nurses, looking to what infants are desirous of, make a conjecture by their presenting to them something. For they think they correctly offer that, on which being presented the children are silent ; but incorrectly that, at which it sheds tears or cries out. For in the case of children tears and cries are the indications of what they love and hate, (and are) signs by no means lucky. Now this period is not less than three years, a not small portion of life to pass through badly or not badly."*

* *Ibid.,* p. 255.

Then the conversation goes on, indicating that neither the pursuit of pleasure, nor the entire avoidance of pain should be attempted.

"Nor let him permit any other person, old or young, male or female, to suffer the same thing with us, and, as far as *he is able, the newly-born the least of all. For all the manners are, through custom,* implanted in all the most powerfully at that period. And further still, if I were not about to appear to be jesting, I would say, that one ought to attend to women, who are carrying anything in the womb, the most of all during that very year, so that the person pregnant may neither enjoy pleasures numerous and violent, nor, on the other hand, feel pains, but live through that period, preserving a line of conduct benignant, and good-tempered, and mild."*

"*Athen.:* If then in the case of a boy and girl of three years old, any one should bring these matters accurately to an end, and make use of what has been said in not a careless manner, they will be of no small advantage to those recently brought up. But there will be a need of sports for the *habits of the soul* at three, and four, and five, and even six years of age. But we must already remove them from luxury, by chastising them, not in an ignominious manner, but, as we said on the subject of slaves, by chastising not with insults so as to encourage an angry feeling in them, when so chastised, nor a feeling for licentiousness by

* *Ibid.,* pp. 256-7.

I

suffering them to go unpunished, we must do the same in the case of the free-born. Now the sports of persons of that age are self-produced; and which, when they come together, they almost invent themselves. . . . After six years of age let each sex be separated."*

Burges, in a note, says that whatever may have been the case with Greece in the time of Plato, in other countries and more recent periods the sports of children, so far from being invented by themselves, have been handed down from age to age; and as Paley remarked, while empires have flourished and decayed, the sports of children have remained unchanged by time; for they still ride on sticks, and play at odd and even, as Horace tells us they did in his day; and make horses and carts out of orange peel, as Aristophanes states they did more than 2000 years ago.

Then the discourse flows on upon education. The appropriation of so large a space in Plato's graphic description of childhood in his day—to the discussion of errors to be avoided, and the methods to be adopted for a judicious development of the young, cannot fail to impress any one who studies the subject at all.

ROMAN CHILDREN.

Like the Greeks, the Romans regarded childhood mainly as a necessary preliminary introduction to a manhood, in which the orator, the legislator, the

* *Ibid.*, pp. 258-9.

warrior, should live to make his mark on his age, and possibly fill a brilliant page in the history of the Roman empire.

If the Greeks developed the man of intellectual culture—the logician, the poet, the lover of pleasure, the artist of purest ideal in physical beauty and of powerful and varied emotion—the Roman training produced men of practical energy—men who gloried in oratory, and above all, men who would lead armies to victory, men who could make roads all over the empire and found lasting settlements.

We know something of the "stuff" out of which men are formed, but we have very little definite knowledge of the mode by which that stuff was shaped.

The mother's influence over the child was great. She was the worthy companion of her husband. In early times the children sat at table with their parents, and would listen, in respectful silence, to the conversation on the services their father had rendered to the State. They were allowed to accompany their fathers to the senate, and learned to be quiet, or to speak at the proper time. The rod was almost too well known to the children. At least so thought Horace, the pupil of Orbilius Pupillus, who immortalized his cross-grained master in his verse.

At the age of seven the child was handed over to the *grammatistes*, or *literator*, to acquire the art of reading and writing.

The wisdom and tenderness of Quintilian are notice-

I 2

able in his sympathy with children, as it comes out in his observations on the teachableness of youth in general.   He remarks, farther, that if the promise of youth often remains unfulfilled, it is due rather to defective education, than to the want of ability in the child.

Quintilian would have the education begun at the very earliest age, and always in a hopeful spirit. Especially does he urge the greatest care in the selection of a nurse; and it is the duty of the pædagogus to correct the faults of the nurse.   Learning must be felt to be a pleasure and not a burden.   If the child discover no aptitude for one kind of study, let him try another.

We get a glimpse of a Roman home from the writings of Cicero, when he alludes to little Tullia getting clamorous for the promised doll which, it appears, Atticus forgot that he was to give her.   Thus affording us a touch of nature that makes the whole (child) world kin !

THE CHILDREN OF INDIA.

A book with this title gives sufficient illustration for our purpose, of the manner of dealing with children in India.   The inferior position of woman explains the difference in the regard for girls as compared with boys.   The girls are nothing, the boys are everything. You may hear a Hindu talk about children *and* girls : as though girls were not children at all, but something not nearly so good.   If you were to ask a father how many children he had, you would generally be told the number of boys only, for they say " girls don't count."

On the birth of a little girl the Hindus conclude that the gods must have been very angry, as the explanation of their withholding a boy.

When a boy is born, festivities, rejoicings and presents mark the event: on the birth of a girl there is no bell-ringing, there are no presents, no messengers of good news.

A Hindu gentleman has said that—" Honour thy father and thy mother" is the first commandment to the Hindus.

The children are taught that the gods hate them, and that they may hate their gods.

Until five or six years old the boys and girls live together, and very much in the same way.

The girls have no lessons to learn ; the mothers cannot teach them. Until very recently, it was thought absurd to try to teach girls or women to read. The girls have no occupation, no reading, no pictures, no needlework. The men and boys do that. They spend much time in doing their mother's hair, for Hindu ladies think a great deal of their hair, and like to show plenty of it. They enjoy listening to stories. They learn to *cook*. The one thing they are taught to hope and pray for is a nice husband. The girl must be married before she is ten years old. The boys stay at home after marriage—not the girls, whose mothers-in-law are often a terror to them.

In the zenanas they talk about their jewels to their visitors, but never about their husbands.

THE CHILDREN OF PERSIA.

The following sketch is mainly compiled from two original sources, one from the pen of a Nestorian Christian lady who is living and working with her husband in the education of the children of Persia ; the other from a Kurd, whose father was a Kurdish Molla (Mohammedan priest), and who since his conversion to Christianity has suffered much in maintaining his Christian faith.

Suppose we enter a house in a Persian town in which has just arrived a new baby. Boys and girls in our English homes are alike welcome. But here a marked difference is observable between the reception of a boy and a girl. If a boy, every face beams with delight. For days the members of the family circle and neighbours keep holiday and indulge in festivities, mid the strains of musicians. When the musicians learn that a girl is born, they go away disappointed. Friends bring presents. And the individual who carries the good news that a son is born, to the father, receives a handsome gift. How different in the case of a daughter ! Every face is clouded. Curses rest upon her inoffensive head from the hour of her birth.

Motherhood brings with it a love for the child, a characteristic, says our Kurdish friend, that distinguishes the Persian women.

It is the natural affection only of a father which provides for the needs of his girl, otherwise fathers are sure that what they spend on a girl is lost. For example,—one of their great kings Shah Abbas once asked a gardener how much he earned a day. He answered tenpence. The Shah enquired how he spent that. He replied, he owed a man twopence a day, and lent twopence to another ; he threw twopence into the sea, and spent the remaining fourpence on himself and his wife.

Shah Abbas told him he could understand giving twopence back to the man to whom he owed it, but why he lent money while he was in debt, and why he should be so foolish as to throw away money he could *not* understand. The man said that he meant the twopence he paid back was spent on his father, who was old and unable to work; and the twopence which he lent was spent on his son, whom he expected when he grew up would help him as he had helped *his* father ; and the twopence he threw into the sea he spent on his daughters, thus showing that girls are considered of no account.

When a poor little baby is born it is wrapped, according to the custom of the country, in swaddling bands, and a little cap is placed on its head, which is bound round very tightly with a handkerchief. On the day of its birth seven onions are put on an iron rod, and each day one of these is thrown away until the child is seven days old, and round the bed of the

mother and child, which is on the floor, are placed
swords and guns in order that "All" (evil spirits)
which are supposed to be the enemies of the mother
and child, should not come near and kill them; and
till the seventh night the lamps are never put out
during the night.   Children in Persia are never bathed
till they are one year old.

When a child is about a month old, after the Astron-
omers or the Koran have been consulted, and a lucky
hour has been selected, they put it in a cradle, and
bind its legs and arms tightly down with bandages to
the cradle, which is something like a shallow box on
two rockers.   The box is fitted with cushions so that
the child's body is on a level with the top of the box.
A bandage is tied over its eyes so that the poor little
thing is obliged to be quite motionless, with aching
back, it cries and cries, until the mother finishes her
work or returns from her bath.

As a rule the mothers nurse their own children.
They carry the babe strapped to the back while about
their daily duties.   And here, as everywhere else, the
children reflect the disposition, character, and apti-
tudes of the parent.

The little Persian babes are left entirely to their own
resources.   They are not indulged with toys, or games.
Nothing is done to amuse them.   The only occupation
left to interest them is eating.   This is their only joy.

As they grow up, however, little boys, will often
amuse themselves.   They talk about their father's

sheep, and seem to find a pleasure in alluding to " my father's buffalo ; my father's cow." At this age they will gather sticks, and build huts, and act the shepherd. They soon acquire bad habits, and quarrel and fight with one another. Their idea of God becomes associated with swearing, and taking God's name in vain is a common characteristic of the children of parents who know not and care not for God.

The games of little girls at this age are called " lucklooshy." They are played with five stones. These are collected when the children are quite small, and are treasured up till they can use the stones in various ways, as children do knuckle-bones in England.

There are no shops at which the girls can buy dolls. But the instinct of the mother prompts the little one to manufacture its own baby out of a piece of stick and some rags. They also find great amusement in making tiny clay vessels ; forming an oven, and baking their own cakes. They are thus busy at the age of five or six.

At this tender age, the children of cruel mothers are compelled to work very hard, carrying food upon their little backs, to those who may be working upon the farm ; sometimes nursing the baby, or rocking the cradle.

A little girl is taught to swear by the name of her brother. They are expected now to do services for their father and brother. At seven they are not considered too young to do the work of a woman.

Brothers are always up in the morning with the life and bustle of the farm. The little boys sit upon the yoke of the oxen. Others learn to be masons or carpenters, beginning at a very early age. There are very few schools for them other than the school of practical life.

They are really anxious to be instructed, for they are a very intelligent race. Religion is inherent in their nature. Every Mohammedan believes there is a God.

Their personal ambition leads them to seek and to possess a good name, and this quality manifests itself at the age of six or seven. Thus they give great honour to pens, ink, and paper, and look upon these things as holy.

Where a few schools have been opened, a remarkable advance is perceptible. As yet the majority of the inhabitants consider it quite out of place to educate a woman, and therefore very few of the women can read at all.

At the age of seven every girl begins to learn to sew and do fancy work, and this fills up most of her time until she is married.

The manners of the Persians are noticeable. Should a stranger come into the house, the little girl must stand all the time. She prepares the visitors' pipes; in winter weather she has to remove their outdoor garments, and carry water for their ablutions. In fact, the Persian girl is a girl no more after she is eight or nine years of age. In the evening she must always be busy at her distaff and spindle, affording nineteenth century illustrations of the pre-Christian era when Solomon commended the virtuous women, or the still earlier time when the cloth was being spun for the Tabernacle.

A mother kisses her son, but she rarely kisses her daughter. She does not think that her girl has a heart. The sister is trained to lavish her attentions on her brother; the love is not reciprocated. The best of everything is reserved for the boys and men.

Where the Gospel has been proclaimed and received, all this is changed. The home life is moulded in love and unity. The contrast between such a home and the home of a mother who has actually been seen to crush her little girl under her very feet, must be strange indeed.

The people are steeped in superstition. And the poor Persian children are terrified by the fearful things they learn. They are taught to believe in genii or demons, and there is a chapter devoted to these genii in the Koran, and some people are believed to influence them. Parents and others are constantly speaking about genii to the children, and think they are every-where; they teach them to say " Bismellah " (in the name of God) in order that the genii should depart.

Children are not fed regularly, and if a child after a late supper has nightmare, and cries out in the night, they say the genii have affected him. The parents run

off to the priest for a prayer ("I have written a good
many of these prayers myself," writes my friend, "having once been a Mohammedan priest") to drive the
genii away.

Persian children are dressed just like grown-up
people, there are no dresses specially devised for children.   Little girls are covered with a chader, which
is a black silk or cotton sheet.   A white veil covers
the face, it has tiny pin-holes over the eyes and nose.
They wear besides a garment which is like loose
trousers.   Boys dress like their fathers.   Children
are compelled to sit and act like grown-up people.   If
they walk or run about a room, like English children,
they are punished.   The chader and veil are worn only
when they go out.

Among the nobility men and women are employed
to teach them how to behave like grown-up people.
Boys are miniature men, and girls miniature women.
There is really no child-life in Persia.   But few
schools, and these, unlike our own where all is done
to make school-days bright and happy, are dull and
uninteresting.   The children are made to repeat a
sentence over and over again, parrot fashion, something like this :—" Kaf lam push kul aooyo," and they
do not even understand the meaning of the words.
They must read the whole of the Koran, 114 chapters,
in this parrot fashion, without understanding it, before
they read any other book.   This tedious reading of an
unknown tongue takes four or five years.

In winter they must get up very early in the morning. A bag of charcoal in one hand, a little napkin
containing food in the other, they (the boys) start for
school. If late they are whipped. Each boy has a
pot (like a flower-pot) in which he puts his charcoal,
and puffs and puffs, until it is red-hot; then places a
cushion close to it, on which he sits, his Koran on his
lap, moving his body backwards and forwards all the
time repeating the monotonous words of the Koran.
The schoolroom is a small one, with a small door, and
two little holes in the walls to serve for windows; both
door and holes are closed in winter, so there is no
ventilation whatever. The fumes of the charcoal and
the closeness of the room, where so many children are
gathered, causes headache and makes them nervous
and feverish.

They have no recreation hour and no play, and often
school begins at sunrise and continues till sunset. In
summer time it is better for them, for then doors can
be opened and fresh air let in.

If a boy gets tired of this tedious routine and runs
away from the school, or is unable to master the difficult Arabic verses of the Koran, they are bastinadoed—
a very cruel form of punishment. If they get tired of
the motion of constantly moving backward and forward and rest, they are struck with a stick on the
shoulders. There are no holidays during the whole
year, except on Fridays, which is the Sabbath in
Persia. A master of such a school himself knew some

children who, after eight years learning in the way described, could not tell one letter from another. No wonder that with such a system of education one finds in Persia among one thousand men, perhaps but one who is able to read and write; and among one hundred who *can* read and write only one can do so correctly.

No education of any sort is provided for girls, except among the rich whose daughters are sometimes taught to read the Koran, which is, among Mohammedans, considered a meritorious thing to do. Village boys have a happier life, as they are free from school altogether and spend their days attending cattle.

Children in Persia are taught very early to hate Christians and the Jews, especially the latter, and think of them as unclean. On their way to school, or shops, they torment the Jewish boys and girls by striking them on their heads, stoning them, &c.; and are encouraged to do this by grown-up people.

THE CHILDREN OF CHINA.

The advent of a little boy in a Chinese family is an event. There never was such a fine baby born! What compliments pass! What rejoicings take place! But as in so many other countries, the little girls are great mistakes, and it goes badly with them. The first three days they lie on some rags on the floor. This is the preface to the sad story of their lives.

When three days old the baby is washed with charmed water, for luck; in this water there are pepper, dates, walnuts, soap, chips of acacia wood, and other ingredients, good for washing off the baby's outside skin. Then it is washed in more water, in which have been put some "cash," chestnuts, dates and silver. This washing is designed to secure riches for the child when it shall have grown up. Then a large plaster is put on the baby, made of pitch and a plant called mugwort. The object of this is to prevent its having any aches or pains. After this the skin is smeared with white of egg to give it a good complexion, and then it is beaten on the hip with an onion to make it clever.

For fourteen days, and sometimes for a longer period, the baby undergoes the ceremony of "binding the wrists." A piece of red cord, about two feet long, so as not to interfere with the infant's freedom is tied round each of the wrists and fastened. Some children have a few old cash tied to the cord. Some have a red string without any cash. Others have silver toys, as well as cash, tied round their wrists. The charm of the cord is that it will keep them from being naughty afterwards, preventing their being frightened, and throwing their arms about. Evil spirits are to be kept away by the cash; and the toys are to make it a happy child.

When a child is a month old all its hair is shaven off. If the baby is a boy, the relatives and friends are

invited to a feast the day he is shaven, and presents
pour in on the lucky little fellow, one of the gifts
always being a plate with " Long life, honours, and
happiness," engraved upon it.

After the first washing a baby is not put into the
water for a year. It is considered dangerous. Its face
and hands are wiped with a damp cloth ; the rest of
its little body goes dirty. Its head is shaven often to
increase the growth of the hair, and when an inch or
two long it is plaited into a tiny tail on the top of the
head with a bit of silk.

The infant never gets any kisses. The mother
smells its face instead of kissing it. Instead of ex-
claiming "what a darling !" the mother says : "how
nice you smell !"

It is not often that a girl will get the fondling that
a mother gives to her boy. Alas ! multitudes of girls
are destroyed as soon as they are born ; their inhuman
parents would rather kill them than have to feed them.
They are often drowned like kittens; and with greater
cruelty still, they are sometimes burned alive.

How is the intelligence of a boy first addressed ?
and how is the bent of his genius first discovered?
At about three months old, he has several objects
placed before him—a pair of shears, a pair of scales,
a measure, a mirror, a pencil, some ink, paper, books,
and other things, and from what he first happens to
touch, it is inferred what he is going to be when he
becomes a man. If he put his hand on a book or a

pen, they say he will be a great scholar; if he touch the scales, he is destined to be a successful merchant.

The child's first instruction is in the worship of idols and its dead relations and spirits. They are taught to work as soon as they can walk. This develops a gravity of demeanour which is characteristic of the Chinese. Before visitors children are reverential. If a visitor ask to see the boys, they are sent for, and on entering the room they kneel down before the visitor, and knock their heads on the floor several times, and then they get up and stand facing him, but some distance off. And this is good behaviour in which the Chinese take great pride.

The Chinese are great at gambling, and as their children have few games or toys, but are taught that they must behave like gentlemen, they soon acquire the gentlemanly habit of gambling with cards and dominoes. Perhaps a less objectionable accomplishment for a gentleman is the making and flying of kites, for which they have a world-wide reputation.

Obedience is a fine characteristic of a child; and the Chinese display this virtue long after our English children have put it away as a childish thing.

With the prevailing superstition of the parents, the children are soon infected. The following story illustrates this, but it also tells of something better. The tenderness and sympathy of a little girl were brought out through her unintentionally causing the death of two dragon-flies while playing with them. This so

K

preyed on her mind that she fell ill, and for a time lost her reason. Her parents were much concerned and being as superstitious as the child, sent for the Buddhist and Taoist priests to cure their child, but the louder they chanted the worse the child became, till they feared she would die. The news of the trouble and its cause spread, and a native gentleman who was a scholar, hearing of it, went to the house and told her parents that he had knowledge of what we call "the black art," and could restore their little girl if they would allow him to do so. They thanked him, and he ordered the whole gang of priests away, and when quiet was restored went in to see the child and told her that by his arts he had captured the spirits of the two dragon-flies and imprisoned them in two paper ones which he would show her, and that if she burnt incense and made her prostrations to the paper ones containing the spirits of the dead, they would leave off troubling her.

The child did so and recovered from her fears and was soon well again.

The parents offered him money and thanks, but he said, " you foolish people, it is you with your ignorance and nonsense that have hurt the little girl and nearly killed her, not the dead flies. I have no such power as you suppose, but by deceit have undone the harm that your foolish teaching has done the child."

Chinese girls, while yet quite young, are set to work. One of their first occupations is pasting bits of old rags to boards, till they are about as thick and strong as pasteboard. These are put to dry in the sun, and then the rag is pulled off the boards and cut up into soles for the common kind of shoes.

English children as well as grown-up people are generally very polite to strangers. The Chinese are polite at home; they are ready to give up their favourite toys, their cherished seat, their most prized books to others, and they do not make themselves miserable by these little acts of self-denial.

Every boy means to be a learned man; learning comes before wealth. Paper, ink, slabs, and brushes are called the four precious things. Thus the faculties of the boys are encouraged.

This story of a little boy, who was ambitious to become a learned man, is authentic. He was so poor, he could not afford a candle, and the evening was his only time for study. His neighbours in the next house enjoyed the light of candles. A chink in the wall allowed a streak of light to shine upon the boy's book, and thus was he able to pursue his studies.

Another boy depended for his evening light on a fire-fly shut up in a bottle, and by this light he used to read.

A boy, who was always falling asleep over his lessons, would keep himself awake by tying his pig-tail to a beam in his room, so that when he nodded he would wake up by a pull at his pig-tail.

As we find in other countries where woman is de-

K 2

graded, the men undergo examinations from which women are excluded.

Ancient institutions and customs are perpetuated from generation to generation. And children—cabined, cribbed, confined—have a poor chance of healthy development of mind on the lines of nature or grace.

CHILDHOOD IN THE DARK CONTINENT.

The following statements touching childhood in Africa are mainly from "*The Children of Africa.*"

"Lander when he was in Africa saw a mother sell her little girl for a necklace. She was not a baby either, so it was not to save carrying her, that her mother wanted to sell her. The poor little girl clung to her mother's knees, saying, 'Oh, mother, do not sell me. What will become of me? What will become of you when you get old, if you let me go away from you? Who will fetch your corn and milk? Who will pity you when you die?' But the mother took no notice, and the poor little girl was sold, and all for the sake of a necklace. Among the Fantees, fathers and mothers pawn their children. Husbands pawn their wives too, and even themselves. If the person pawned is a woman or girl, the man who takes her can be just as cruel to her as he likes."

"You must not think that all West African mothers are bad ones. Some of them love their children very much, and their children love them."

"Another very cruel thing that is done in West Africa, and in other parts too, is that if two little babies are born at the same time they are killed, because it is thought unlucky to have twins. On the Niger, when twins are born, they are killed directly and thrown away, and nobody is ever allowed to speak about them."

"In some parts of West Africa not only twins are killed, but also all boys and girls whose top teeth come through before their bottom ones."

"In Lower Guinea, as soon as a child is born, the news is told in the street by the crier in a loud voice, so that every one may know. Then someone in another part of the town answers the cry, and promises that the people of the town will receive the child amongst them, and that it shall be treated as if it belonged to them. Then a crowd collects in the street, and the baby is brought out and shown. A basin of water is brought too, and the head man of the town or family sprinkles some water on the baby, gives it a name, and says he hopes it may live to be old, to be rich, and to have many children of its own, or something of that sort. Most of the people in the crowd do the same as the head man, till the poor baby is quite wet through. All who help in this sprinkling promise that they will be friends of the baby. The people say they do not know what was the beginning of this custom, nor whether it has any meaning."

"The children in Lower Guinea are taught to be very respectful to old people."

" Among the Zulus and most other tribes in South Africa, the parents are very glad when a girl is born, because they expect to get a good price for her from the man who marries her."

" When she is fourteen or fifteen a girl is called grown-up, and then, instead of being more useful, as you would expect, she is allowed to be just as lazy as she likes for a few years, and in some parts of the country spends her time in lying on the ground in the sun, gossiping, dancing, or at the best, making belts, necklaces, bracelets, and rings with beads. She lives this idle life till she gets married, which is not generally till she is eighteen or twenty, though in some tribes the girls marry younger. . . . . She will have no time to be lazy after that. She will have to put on a leather petticoat, cut the front part of her hair close to her head, make a chignon at the back dyed red (this is the sign of a married woman) and set to work to get food for her husband."

" The Bushmen are not all kind to their wives and children. A father often nearly kills his children if he is angry with them, or if they are not a nice shape, or even if they want food. The children are often smothered or strangled, or thrown away in the desert to be starved or eaten by wild beasts. Even the mothers are no better. Sometimes if a lion is heard roaring at the mouth of a cave (you remember the Bushmen's huts are really caves), a father or mother will throw their baby to it to make it quiet. The mothers generally take no care of their children after they are able to crawl about by themselves. If a mother dies when her child is still younger than this, the child is buried alive with her."

"The Barotsi, who live north of Bechuanaland, have some very cruel customs with the children. At very important times they cut off the fingers and toes of a little child, and sprinkle some of the blood on the boat or house that the king is going to use, and then toss the child into the Zambesi river."

It is recorded of missionaries in Africa that when entering a fresh district and seeing the alarm on the faces of natives, and the preparations for war at the sight of the white-faced strangers, peace and content (re-assurance ?) and a sense of security will immediately reign amongst the men when the missionary puts forth his wife and child for them to do what they like with them.

ARAB CHILDREN.

From a work on *Domestic Life in Palestine* we give a glimpse of Arab child life, with some of its special characteristics.

During the absence of the Consul, Miss Rogers was visited by two little girls of the Sakhali family who came to her, saying, "Oh, Miriam, peace be upon you. We have thought that you must be sad and lonely. . . . may he return to you soon and in safety ! ". . . . . They

were very clever, quick children; and though only
eight and nine years old, they could already make
bread and prepare many simple dishes. They were
surprised that Miss Rogers had not been taught how
to cook; it is the chief point in the education of an
Arab girl. On being summoned away from the children, whom she had been amusing and instructing from
her workbox, and the children being told that she must
go, they said :—"We are glad that you will to-day see
the Consul; but we are sorry you are going away from
us; go in peace."

Another story, from the same book, illustrates the
influence of children.

"Little Nimhr, the son of the Agha, arrived; he was
about seven years old. He came bounding into the
room, and was soon wrapped in the folds of his father's
scarlet cloak and covered with kisses and caresses.
I was struck by the change in the somewhat stern
aspect of Salihh Agha. He was full of tenderness and
demonstrative affection for his little son, an ugly boy,
but of that piquant description of ugliness which is
sometimes so attractive . . . . . He showed in every
action that he was accustomed to be noticed and
lovingly treated."

The following picture of the freedom of the younger
children in the presence of an affectionate father, and
the restrained behaviour of an educated elder daughter
of the same father, throws light on the family life.

"His, Saleh Bek's, children unconsciously proved

to me that they were accustomed to be caressed by him, for they clustered round him lovingly, and little Saïd was especially demonstrative. He said coaxingly, 'O, my father, may I go to see the house of the English lady? it is her wish that I should go.' Asmé, his eldest daughter, scarcely spoke a word, and sat sedately still and impassive; and the face which a few minutes before had seemed to me so beautiful with vivacity and cheerfulness looked quite unattractive. It seems to me to be a part of Oriental etiquette for the elder children to preserve a kind of grave decorum in the presence of a father, the younger children alone are free to show their natural feelings, and demonstrative affection is regarded as childish and undignified."

Old Testament facts are confirmed by the present habits of the Arabs in Palestine. The East is stationary. Many of the practices of the Arabs of to-day are as old as the book of Genesis and the time of the Patriarchs.

NEW GUINEA.

While at this section of the book, Mrs. Chalmers, the wife of a Christian missionary in New Guinea, brought under the writer's notice some interesting facts connected with their life among the " Savages."

During the first year of a child's life the mother is expected to devote herself entirely to her offspring and it is therefore necessary for a second wife to attend to

the cultivation of the ground, which is her particular
right, and prepare food for the husband.

Their affection is remarkable; and the father shares
the solicitude of the mother. The gentleness and
tenderness of the fathers is such as one observes in the
Japanese, who enjoy the nursing of the children in
their dinner hour as the best part of the meal.

The boy's early education and amusement consist
in the training of the eyes and limbs, especially in the
use of the assegai and the bow and arrow. The career
of a warrior is placed before their ambition as the
great object of their lives. As the child grows older,
he is passed through several stages of his progress
towards manhood, each stage being marked by an
initiatory rite, and celebrated by a festival. The
children, boys and girls, are taught dancing,—the
sexes always being divided, while the two parties are
in sight of each other. The mothers dress the children with flowers and artistically arranged leaves. The
attention of Mr. and Mrs. Chalmers was drawn to the
children, while watching their movements. "That's
my boy," "That's my beauty," might be heard with
delighted exclamations. As the boys grow up, the
initiatory mysteries suggest some severe if not cruel
rites, but Mr. Chalmers has never penetrated the
secret. They are shut up at the age of twelve in sacred
custody of old men: no woman is allowed to go near
the enclosure.

These good missionaries have won the affection

and respect of the natives. Our artificial, unnatural civilization in Mr. Chalmer's estimation is not to be preferred to the simple, free and natural civilization of the savages ! He knows them, and trusts them, and he goes about among them without fear. One day Mrs. Chalmers missed a table cloth. She denounced the thief—would have nothing to do with man or boy, till the table cloth was restored. One boy at length produced it. He said he found it at the bottom of the river. But the coffee stains, &c., upon it refuted the explanation. Still they were glad it was returned, and several devoted converts wiped their tears from their eyes, when they knew they were to be treated as friends again.

The natives usually crowd around, many coming into the sitting room of the missionaries, but while partaking of a meal, they show their delicacy of feeling by withdrawing to the outside, or stopping in the doorway. They have made many of their converts teachers in their school.

According to Figuier, the Patagonians are about the lowest in the scale of humanity. " The existence of a new-born infant is submitted to the (kind ?) consideration of the father and mother, who decide upon its life or death. Should they think fit to get rid of it, it is smothered, and its body carried a short distance, and then abandoned to wild dogs and birds of prey."

Marriage among these nations is a traffic, a barter of various articles and animals for a wife. The woman moreover is burdened with work, whilst the man takes his ease, whenever he is not hunting or engaged in minding the cattle.

THE CHILDREN OF JAPAN.

"The gentleness of Jesus."

"The Gospel of Creation "* it may be difficult to trace among whole nations of savages, so completely has it vanished like a bright morning cloud from their horizon,—so clearly erased, *apparently*, from the tablet of the human heart. Yet it would be more correct, perhaps, to say that " it is hid to them that are lost," and only hidden beneath the rubbish which centuries of perversity, barbarity and brutality have accumulated over it. Bishop Westcott cannot greatly err when he maintains that the incarnation preceded sin : and although sin has marred "the human face divine," the likeness of God is only defaced not destroyed. The fine gold has become dim, but the gold of incarnate Divinity has not all been extracted from the mine of humanity.

One sweet trait of the nature of Christ is His *gentleness*.† It is remarkable that during the eighteen cen-

---

* Vide *Christus Consummator : some Aspects of the Work and Power of Christ in relation to Modern Thought*, by Brooke Foss Westcott, D.D., D.C.L., Bishop of Durham, second edition, 1887.

† "Now I Paul myself intreat you, *by the meekness and gentleness of Christ*, I who in your presence am lowly among you . . . "—2 COR. x. 1.

turies of Christian civilization—especially among theologians,—this tender plant, the gentleness of Christ,
may be sought after and found only as a very rare
specimen. Choked by the bitter weeds of arrogance,
self-assertion, and implied or avowed infallibility, the
gentleness of Jesus seems almost to have been exter-
minated or to have perished. The tendency of offi-
cialism is to wither it, whether in Church or State.
Spiritual power and authority are incompatible. Des-
potism and gentleness have never been twin sisters.
Anathema and meekness do not well up from the same
fountain.

The Gospel of Creation is obscured or "hid" among
the nations who know not God ; but it is not difficult
to trace a line here and there of its primal fulness and
perfection. Nor ought it to surprise us if, among the
heathen, fragments of the precious gift, by Creative
grace, have been preserved. The East will bear its
testimony as well as the West. If the children of
Abraham still nourished the sense of divine *righteousness;* if something of its essential glory survived in the
genius and ideal *beauty* of the Greek ; if its divine *order*
still asserted itself in Roman jurisprudence, why should
we be surprised if vestiges of the primal gospel are discoverable in the life and character of the Japanese ?

There are many points of identity between the
Japanese and the Chinese. The creeds of Buddha and
Confucius have both moulded the religious thought
and life of the two nations. Their priests and pagodas

are alike. Their literature and written language are the same. Till the Chinese men adopted pigtails, the hair of both nations was worn in the same manner. The buildings and junks were till quite recently the same, as also their kinds of food. But it is in a *moral* point of view the Japanese compare most favourably with the Chinese. They are cleanly in their persons and dwellings : intelligent, brave and honourable.

For a remarkable instance of the survival of the Gospel of Creation we may go to Japan. We plume ourselves on our superiority, and lay the flattering unction to our souls that the Japanese are indebted to our European ideas and institutions for their rapid progress in the arts of civilization. Doubtless the Japanese would gratefully and ungrudgingly acknowledge their obligations to Europe. But the power of rapid assimilation is due to their own moral capacity— the receptivity of their gentle natures—their freedom from prejudice and suspicion. No other Asiatic nation has discovered the same plastic quality by which its life could be so readily moulded by the arts of Western Civilization as the Japanese. Their peculiar aptitude for taking on the forms of European life is most striking. How is this? *They have gentle manners.* They are child-like. Explain it how we may, they manifest in their every-day life that beautiful quality which we admire as gentleness. This is *their* cherished inheritance from the Gospel of Creation. It was not a very conspicuous trait in the character of the Goths, the

Vandals or the Huns. Neither the Angles and Saxons, nor the Conqueror, achieved celebrity under the banner of the dove. And the existing nations of Europe and America are far more familiar with the lion, the serpent, the eagle, the dragon, and other rude monsters, than with this tender Paradisaical bird.

But what has all this to do with the children of Japan ? Let us see.

The Japanese are just now debating whether they shall mould their habits on the Christian system of morality, or on science and philosophy. They are *really* divided between the Gospel which they have inherited from Creation, and the gospel of conventional Christianity, as they estimate it from our intercourse with them. If they could really see the Christ putting a little child in the midst, they would feel so thoroughly at home with Him, that the controversy would be at once ended. For childhood lies at the very foundation of their domestic and social life.

We, the professed followers of the meek and gentle Jesus, are simply startled by the public announcements just now being issued under the benign authority of the Mikado. These announcements touch practical, and especially official, life. Did any *Christian* government ever suggest to Count Goto, one of the Japanese ministers, that in the Communications Department— in post-offices and postal savings-banks—" every member of the public, irrespective of social or official position, should be treated with politeness and civility " ?

The same minister further urges the importance ot avoiding all assumption of authority or show of official-dom, in dealing with females, old people, and *those of tender years.* Every official should be "kind and un-assuming to all persons entitled to avail themselves of his services;" and the public, "so far from being rendered reluctant to face the airs of officialdom, should be able to feel that they may always count on ready and polite attention."* The writer once asked a class of 250 children, how they regarded the policeman. Most of them evidently shuddered at the name; and one little girl said she should run away as fast as she could. This may be less discreditable to the police than to parents, who most unfairly threaten the troublesome child with "the policeman" as a stimulus.

Neither through the channels of commerce nor the church can this gentleness be regarded as a European import. If it be not a vestige of that original gospel written on the fleshly table of the heart, what is it? What can it be? That it is not something foreign, now for the first time grafted on the Institutions of Japan, is clear. It is indigenous—not exotic. It is a natural evolution, and no prettier bit of evidence can be adduced than that which modern travellers in the Mikado's domains describe.   .

That the unit of humanity is not the individual but the *family*—man, woman, and child—will not be dis-puted. The formative forces of humanity as expressed

* See *Daily Telegraph*, June 13th, 1889.

in the family life, are not exhausted there. They work from the family to the state, which properly becomes a larger family ; and with practical eyes we are actually seeing, more and more clearly, with the progress of true Christianity, that the nations—all the families of the earth—are members only of one great community—*brethren* of whom the Christ is the One head.

The unity of Japan, in its beautiful social aspects, is based on the family life. Its *natural* history is not to be traced in the enforcement by external authority of a cut and dried extraneous system, forced upon the nation by " a new constitution," but by the working of the leaven of the family unit spreading its benevolent and amiable influence through the ramifications of society.

The following facts, by an English eye-witness, will justify the theory suggested :—

" I never saw people take so much delight in their offspring, carrying them about, or holding their hands in walking, watching and entering into their games, supplying them constantly with new toys, taking them to picnics and festivals, never being content to be without them, and treating other people's children also with a suitable measure of affection and attention. Both fathers and mothers take pride in their children. It is most amusing about six every morning to see twelve or fourteen men sitting on a low wall, each with a child, under two, in his arms, fondling and playing with it, and showing off its physique and intelligence.

L

To judge from appearances, the children form the chief topic at this morning gathering. At night, after the houses are shut up, looking through the long fringe of rope or rattan which conceals the sliding door, you see the father, who wears nothing but a *maro* in 'the bosom of his family,' bending his ugly, kindly face over a gentle-looking baby, and the mother, who more often than not, has dropped the *kimono* from her shoulders, enfolding two children destitute of clothing in her arms. . . . . . . The children, though for our ideas too gentle and formal, are very prepossessing in looks and behaviour. They are so perfectly docile and obedient, so ready to help their parents, so good to the little ones, and, in the many hours which I have spent in watching them at play, I have never heard an angry word, or seen a sour look or act."*

"The village Jrimichi, which epitomizes for me at present the village life of Japan, consists of about 300 houses built along three roads, across which steps in fours and threes are placed at intervals. Down the middle of each a rapid stream runs in a stone channel, and this gives endless amusement to the children, specially to the boys, who devise many ingenious models and mechanical toys, which are put in motion by water-wheels. . . . . . Obedience is the foundation of the Japanese social order, and with children accustomed to unquestioning obedience at home the (school) teacher has no trouble in securing quietness, attention,

* Miss Bird's *Unbeaten Tracks in Japan*, vol. i., p. 140.

and docility. There was almost a painful earnestness in the old-fashioned faces which pored over the school-books; even such a rare event as the entrance of a foreigner failed to distract these childish students. . . . . The mechanical toys, worked by water-wheels in the stream, are most fascinating."

This is followed by a description of a children's party. " One of their games was most amusing, and was played with some spirit and much dignity. It consisted in one child feigning sickness, and another playing the doctor, and the pompousness and gravity of the latter, and the distress and weakness of the former, were most successfully imitated. Unfortunately the doctor killed his patient, who counterfeited the death sleep very effectively with her whitened face; and then followed the funeral and the mourning. They dramatize thus weddings, dinner-parties, and many other of the events of life. *The dignity and self-posses-sion of these children are wonderful.* The fact is that their initiation into all that is required by the rules of Japanese etiquette, begins as soon as they can speak, so that by the time they are ten years old they know exactly what to do and avoid under all possible circum-stances."*

Let these illustrations suffice in substantiation of the claim we have made on behalf of the children of Japan.

Sir Edwin Arnold gives a pretty picture, in *Scribner's Magazine*, of Japanese children, whose admirable be-

* *Ibid.*, pp. 131-2.

haviour, as he says, really seems absolutely to confute the doctrine of original sin. " They never seem to do any mischief, possibly because there is not much mischief to do. In the houses nothing of any value exists for them to break ; there is nothing they will perpetually be told ' not to touch.' The streets almost entirely belong to them (there is practically no horse traffic in Tokio), and yet, although they may do almost anything there they never seem to do anything wrong. Everybody is friendly to them ; every fifth shop is full of toys and dolls, and sweetstuff of strange device, ingredients, and colour, for their delectation. Their innocent ways and merry chatter render every quarter pleasant." And they are the opposite of useless in the domestic economy, these black-eyed youngsters. "We shall see hundreds of children, not more than five or six years of age, carrying, fast asleep, strapped on their small shoulders, the baby of the household."

The children of Madagascar.

The state of civilization and the moral condition of a people may, to a great extent, be measured by the reception given to that little item we call *a baby*. A nation addicted to infanticide, to contempt for children, will be characterised by barbarity, and their country must be reckoned among the dark places of the earth.

How do the Malagasy welcome the little stranger ?

Thus: "Hail! God has blessed you! God has given you a successor, so we are come to bring you a little money to buy shrimps for the baby's mother." The baby's friends reply: "May you live long, may you be long protected from witchcraft, may you, too, have babies born to you! and as for the money you have brought, what is that to us? It is your coming to visit us that makes us glad; but since it is customary, we thank you; may God bless you!" None of these visitors who come crowding into the house when a baby is born ask to look at the little new-comer; that would be considered quite improper; but after asking whether it is a boy or a girl, they sit and chat for a while, and then take their leave, the women often carrying off a quantity of dried beef in their lamba, a present from the baby's father."

The belief in witchcraft and in evil spirits in Madagascar is, alas! most profound, and it brings the Malagasy quite up to the level of a British superstition which still lurks about the Church as well as the rural districts of our country. Hence children born on unlucky days, have been put to death by thousands. Prompted by their affection for their children and their alarm at the evils threatening their lives, and considering, in their ignorance that these evils could only be averted by death, they were driven to infanticide.*

* An English Christian father, out of the tenderest affection of his heart, expressed himself, in the hearing of his children, as wishful that his own offspring might die young, that they might be saved from sin-

" Sometimes, however, the child was not put to
death at once, but placed out at the village gate, or
at the entrance of an ox-pit in the yard outside the
house, just at the time when the cattle were being
driven home for the night. If the oxen all passed by
without touching it, the evil fates which had hung over
the child's life were supposed to be removed, and it
was taken home again, *with great rejoicing*. A very
interesting story was told me by one of my scholars
how on one occasion a little child, belonging to a slave
woman of theirs, was placed at the gate of an ox-pit,
when seven oxen were being driven home in the evening. The first on coming to the place where the baby
lay, put its nose down and smelt it, or as the Malagasy
say 'kissed' it, for their kissing consists in nose-rub-
bing, then at one bound jumped right over it and down
into the pit below. The second came and smelt it and
leapt over it in the same way; the third came and did
just the same, and the fourth, and so on until the
seventh, and it too jumped right over the little one
without harming it in the least. How the poor
mother's heart must have beat with hope and fear as
she saw one after another of the huge beasts come up
and thus take compassion on her little child! It is
said that the present prime minister of Madagascar
was put out in this way to be trodden by the cattle,

ning and from the destructive consequences of sin. The writer also
recalls the case of a Christian English mother, goaded to madness by
the dread for her child of eternal torments, drowning it in a water-butt.

but he likewise escaped, and has lived to rise to great power and has been the husband of three Queens of Madagascar."

Might there not be as intense a maternal affection in the Malagasy mother as there was in the mother of Moses, whose successful attempt to save the boy will be carried down the stream of time to the end of the world?

The greatest store is put upon a first-born child. The first time the baby is taken into the open air, when it is a month old, is an important ceremony. So is also the first hair-cutting, at the age of three months, when the relatives and friends of the family assemble. If the parents are sufficiently well-to-do, one or two or more oxen have been killed, and part of the meat put on the fire to cook, and part cut up to be given to each guest when departing . . . . The hair-cutting is proceeded with, with due formality: the hair removed from the child's head is carried off to the doorway, and placed under the threshold, and a prayer for good-luck is offered. On the occasion of the first hair-cutting the child receives a name.

The little ones run about naked till about three, then they are put into a little *akanje*, or shirt-like garment.

Children are very early set to useful occupations. While the slave or the mother is getting the supper ready, the father will often tell the children stories or get them to play at riddles.

Charms and medicine reveal the superstitious character of the Malagasy people. Prohibited things are
called *fàdy*. Thus a little child about a year old must
not be called good-looking or fat, but be spoken of as
ugly, or called a little pig, or a little dog. An old man
explained that the fear of the child being haunted by
ghosts was at the bottom of the practice.

To give a young child an egg to eat is *fàdy*. The
reason given is that they are both eggs, and it cannot
be right that one egg should eat the other. Kissing a
child's hand is to be carefully avoided, as it is said the
youngster so treated wil become selfish, and will beg
for anything it sees. So we learn that selfishness is
not deemed a great virtue. Nor are they encouraged
to repent of a generous action, for they are warned
that if they want back anything they have given away,
they might cause the death of their mother.

Though the language is so copious in words which
express the superstition of the people, it contains but
one word which signifies *God*,—the intuition of a
higher being.

The success of Christian missions in the education
given in schools is remarkable. The spiritual possibilities of the children are developed quickly, while the
adults, loaded with superstitions and often hardened in
selfishness and sin, are difficult to reach.

M. Lobrichon's well-known picture "*Il était une fois....*" is, with the permission of Messrs. Boussod, Valadon and Co., reproduced here on account of the various phases of child-life which it records, and the striking character which it depicts, not of one child alone, but of each one of the group. The motherly authority of the narrator; the appreciative interest of the eldest listener, with the absorbed attention evinced in the suspended needle-work. The wondering meditative mood of the next, and the least of a funny enquiring turn of mind; the artist not failing in the attitudes of the children, nor the surroundings of the somewhat humble home.

CHAPTER V.

THE CHILD OF ART.

IT is a remarkable fact, that in both ancient literature and art, childhood counted for very little. With the poets a child is a *rara avis*. And with the artists the child is a *little* old man. The estimate of a child was not Wordsworth's—"father of the man," but only *possible man*. The child grew in interest only as he approached the state of manhood.

Childhood is the period of weakness, and it is its weakness which lends to infancy its wonderful pathos. In the character of the lively Greek or the prosaic Roman, strength of mind and of muscle drew forth admiration and awoke the strenuous endeavour to excel.

Take the sculpture of the Greek. Ideal strength seems to assert itself at least as fully as ideal beauty— and only the beauty of man and woman is thought worthy of the chisel of the artist.

If only mothers had been artists, what pictures would have come down to us from early times!

Certainly there are no indications during the best period of Greek art of childhood as a special study for the sculptor. The beauty of children seems to be passed by for the more stately beauty of men and women. The Greeks were sensuous, and the more fully developed form of a Venus had an attraction which the little child utterly failed to excite. To the Greek the family was bound together by ties far inferior in strength to that of personal friendship, and not nearly so sacred as that of country.

The story of Niobe comes down to us through Homer and various classical authors, who differ much as to the details. According to the common story, which represents her as a daughter of Tantalus, she was the sister of Pelops, and married to Amphion, King of Thebes, by whom she became the mother of many sons and daughters. Proud of the number of her children she deemed herself superior to Leto, who had given birth to two children only. Apollo and Artemis, indignant at such presumption, slew all the children of Niobe. For nine days their bodies lay in their blood, without anyone burying them, for Zeus had changed the people into stones; but on the tenth day the gods themselves buried them. Niobe herself, who had gone to Mount Sipylus, was metamorphosed into stone, and *even thus continued to feel* the calamity with which the gods had visited her. The story of Niobe and her children was frequently taken as a subject of ancient art.

The most celebrated was the group which filled the pediment of the temple of Apollo Socianus, at Rome; and which was found at Rome in the year 1583. This group is now at Florence, and consists of the mother who holds her youngest daughter on her knees, and thirteen statues of her sons and daughters besides the pædagogus of the children.

This story reflects the character of the mother and her devotion to her children at a very early period.

We ransack the treasures of Greek art for a little child almost in despair. But Praxiteles is not dead. He lives in Hermes, the tender guardian of young children, the god who when a child is forsaken of father or mother, takes him up and tends him.

The young god Dionysos, child of the fruitful earth and the bright sunshine, offspring of Semele and the golden shower of Zeus, was just such a forsaken little one. This tender woman-hearted Hermes evokes our admiration and our love, without awe or fear. Even the child Dionysos has no fear. His little hand is laid trustfully on the shoulder of Hermes.

Miss J. E. Harrison* relates the discovery by the German excavators at Olympia in 1877, of the statue of Hermes ; but after describing its surpassing beauty, she tells us that Dionysos, so far as beauty goes, is most disappointing. "The hair, the face, the body are not ill-worked ; but stiff and somewhat unpleasant, and wholly unchildlike. As regards mere beauty, we could wish they had never been found."

Pheidias is known for accuracy in minutest details, as well as majesty in his colossal figures. He gave proofs of his skill by making images of minute objects

* *Introductory Studies in Greek Art.*

such as cicadas, bees, and flies—in chasing and en-
graving. But were the children, notwithstanding, beneath his notice ? If imitative art was beneath
Pheidias, was there nothing in infancy to provoke an
effort for the attainment of the ideal beauty of his
inspired genius ? He dwelt among the gods; he
seems to have had no idea of a God incarnate in
an infant.

Roman art was severe   and power in any and every
form they worshipped. The weakness of a little child
made child-life a matter of indifference. It was valuable only for what it might become in after years.

The Italian painters appreciated the beauty of infancy, but their conceptions were developed exclusively
in their endeavours to picture the infant Jesus. The
same may be said of early Flemish art. In Spanish
art we at once recall Murillo's lively beggar boys which
convey the idea to our minds that in him we have an
illustration of one who was devoted to the study of
child-life. But in Spain, where he is certainly seen at
his best, they are the exceptions to the general rule—
such pictures being rarely met with in the country ;
and under his name the many works in other countries
of beggar boys, are said to have been mainly executed
by his followers.

When we come down to Vandyke we see in the
Balbi children an enthusiasm for the glowing loveliness
of an Italian child, though with him it is infrequent
compared with the numerous examples of child-beauty

by Sir Joshua Reynolds, and in the picture galleries of our own day.

How is it that Caldecott has won our admiration and affection too, as the artist of Childhood? What is it that in his subjects and their treatment, has touched all child-like hearts, in young and old alike? It must be the Divine humanity which comes out in the little words of profoundest meaning. "The least of these, my brethren." Is it any exaggeration to say that such artists as Caldecott and Kate Greenaway have done more than most art teachers to inspire and draw out the art instinct in the people? Their secret is truth; no costly elaboration or mechanical trappings—the simple and naked truth.

The growing appreciation of childhood in art is at once the expression and the encouragement of a reverence, a sympathy and a tenderness of compassion known only to those whose highest conceptions and deepest feelings are due to an inspiration whose source is found in the Eternal Love.

To the art of the photographer is justly due the prominence given in recent years to the children. Is it too much to say that portraiture has received a decided impetus through the camera of the photographer? And while children, as a rule, rarely advance beyond a vague and indefinite representation on the canvas of the early masters, photography has developed a child with a well-defined intelligence, and often an intensity of feeling of which ancient art had no conception.

Children have drawn out the genius of the photographic artist, and the photographer, in grateful recognition of the charms of childhood, has done much to bring and to keep the children in the home as prominently as they deserve.

This may horrify some idealists; but popular taste and popular feeling are awakened and developed by photographic portraiture.

CHAPTER VI.

THE CHILDREN OF ISRAEL.

" Give me children, or else I die."—GEN. xxx., 1.

GLIMPSES of the Divine Fatherhood are to be had from very early times among the Jews, and the reflex action of the idea of God as Father is discoverable in the more tender regard for children in subsequent ages.

Plato, as we have seen in the section devoted to the best conceptions of childhood by heathen philosophers, impresses us with his deep interest in the subject. He would have children kept from all that is harmful. He enters into careful study of the training of children, —their religious interests as well as their physical and mental culture,—but that which comes out so prominently in the Jewish conception of religion is utterly wanting in Plato. He claims a great deal of respect for the gods, but he has not a word for what Jews and Christians hold so dear—the *Divine Fatherhood*. This precious truth seems to have been the special gift granted to the children of Abraham.

We find the sacred scriptures gemmed with the endearing terms—"the Father" and "O righteous Father."

The mode of divine manifestation begins with the

idea of righteousness. God's ways are equal. His throne is established in righteousness. Under the form of Law, He made known His ways unto Moses. In harmony with this method, the first commandment runs thus :—*Thou shalt love the Lord thy God with all thy heart.*

God is essentially love ; and as a final testimony to the two fundamental characteristics of the Eternal, our Lord, in the presence of His disciples, apostrophises God thus—*O righteous Father !*

And who could rely on a love that was not righteous? God's love cannot be a mere fickle sentiment ; now hot, now cold. No. *God is love.* And Jesus reveals God, the Father. The New Testament brings out the grand truth, with the clouds and the thunderings and lightnings of Sinai cleared away—and lo ! Jesus with a little child upon His knee !

" But God cannot be the Father of a bad man."

The prodigal son says not only that He can be, but that He is. St. Paul at Athens testified to the same broad fact without qualification or limitation.

A faith in the one God, the God of Abraham, Isaac, and Jacob, is most striking in its manifestation in regard of children, and the religions and civilizations of heathen nations fall into the shade as the practices of those nations in the treatment of children are considered. It is a distinctive feature of Jewish life, through all their history, that children were not regarded as an incumbrance, but as the choicest blessing

God could bestow, and the supreme evidence of Divine favour. The barrenness of a wife was a reproach, and was sometimes considered a sufficient reason for a divorce. True, the birth of a boy was the occasion for more joy than the birth of a girl; but the girl's education was not neglected (Ecclus. xlii. 9, 10). At the hour of birth the father was not present, but he was subsequently admitted, when he took the child upon his knees. If the grandfather were living, he sometimes had this privilege (Gen. l. 23). It was expressly forbidden to make an exhibition of the children, a practice of the Greeks and Romans at which the Jews were horrified.* The mothers nursed their infants themselves, and the Talmud enjoins this as a duty ("Cethubboth" 64 *a*). On the occasion of the weaning of the child Isaac, Abraham made a great feast. And Hagar's greatest distress was occasioned by the apparently inevitable loss of her boy, when "she sat over against him, and lifted up her voice, and wept." (Gen. xxi. 8-17). Palestinian women still prolong the suckling of the child for two or three years; the practice is regarded as a preservative against the maladies incident to the climate.

The recognition of the infant by circumcision when eight days old, must have invested him with a religious interest to the parents, and have touched with an emphatic sacredness the whole family life.

* Philo has a chapter on this subject. See Havel (E.), *Le Judaisme*, p. 437.

M

In Hebrew families the education of the child was a domestic affair; and this would also develop and strengthen those affections which make children so precious.

There were no public schools for children till a century before Christ. Shim'on ben Shattach, the president of the Sanhedrim, brother to Queen Salome, opened the first school in Jerusalem for children. He called it Beth-hassepher (the house of the book). (Jerus., "Cethubboth," VIII. II). The high priest, Jesus ben Gamala, made the founding of schools obligatory; every town was to have a primary school. "Perish the sanctuary," exclaim the Rabbis, in their enthusiasm for the children, "but let the children go to school." (Babyl., "Shabbath" 119 b).

Philo made the study of the Law of the first importance; and Paul reminds Timothy "that from a child thou hast known the Holy Scriptures."

"The mode of education differed widely from ours. As soon as the child could speak his mother taught him a verse of the law. . . . . When the child knew one text he was taught another; then a written scroll of the verses was placed in his hands that he might recite them."*

The importance attached by the Jews to education, and the instruction of the child from a very early age, demonstrate the preciousness of the child. The "Pirke Aboth" (V. 21), some parts of which are cer-

* Stapfer's *Palestine in the Time of Christ.*

tainly anterior to Christianity, thus fixes the various stages of the child's development :—' At five years of age he should commence sacred studies; at ten he should devote himself to the study of tradition; at thirteen he should know and fulfil the commands of Jehovah; at fifteen he should bring his studies to perfection.' "*

Rabbi Judas said :—" If a man does not teach his son a trade it is as if he taught him to steal." (Babyl., " Kiddushin," ch. i.).

At twelve years of age the boys were taken to the Temple; they observed the Torah, and took the name of Bar Micoah; they now fasted regularly, especially on the great day of atonement.

Will it not be found that respect for woman carries with it the greatest regard for children? A virtuous woman (Proverbs of Solomon) is known by her care for her children. As compared with surrounding nations, the honour given to woman among the Jews is very remarkable. Woman is down-trodden by the Arabs to this day.

" On the father," says the Talmud, " devolves the duty of circumcising his son, of teaching him the Law, and of instructing him in a trade."

As illustrative of the honour put upon a child when

---

* " These studies did not amount to much. A knowledge of reading, possibly of writing, and the power of repeating by heart the most important passages of the Torah." Stapfer's *Palestine in the Time of Christ*, p. 144.

he is a boy, the author of *Domestic Life in Palestine*
tells us of a skilful carver in Bethlehem, who was
indebted to H.B.M. Consul Rogers (her brother) for
his start in life and the cultivation of his art.   Miss
Rogers was introduced to his young wife.   She asked
the young mother her name.   She answered " Miriam
is my name."   But her mother said " Not so, she is no
longer Miriam, but Um Yousef (mother of Joseph) for
a son is born unto her whose name is Joseph."

Some of the games of Jewish children are known to
us, of which we get a glimpse in the teachings of Jesus
Himself.   They were fond of playing with tame birds.
(Catullus, ii. 4 ; Plautus, Captiv., Act v. 4, 5).

" As the head of the household returned on the
sabbath eve from the synagogue to his home, he found
it festively adorned, the sabbath lamp brightly burning,
and the table spread with the richest each household
could afford.   But first he blessed each child with the
blessing of Israel."*

" It is when we consider the relations between man
and wife, children and parents, the young and the
aged, that the vast difference between Judaism and
heathenism so strikingly appears.   Even the relationship in which God presented Himself to His people
as their Father, would give peculiar strength and
sacredness to the bond which connected earthly parents with their offspring."†

---

* Edersheim's *Sketches of Jewish Social Life in the days of Christ*,
p. 97.   † *Ibid.*, p. 98.

CHAPTER VII.

THE CHILD OF CHRISTENDOM.

AFTER a study of the child of the Jewish Church, and marking its advantageous position in the family and in the nation, as compared with the offspring of heathen peoples, we may expect that, with a fuller revelation of the Divine Fatherhood, and all that it implies, there will be a further development of the parental appreciation and care for the families of Christian people.

If glimpses of the Divine purity, beauty and sweetness were suggested, though only somewhat obscurely, through the relation of parent and child, in the Israelitish nation, we ought to have impressed upon us still more charming ideas of the attractiveness of the child under the teaching of Jesus, and through Christian training. If children were the riches and glory of social life among the Israelites, their " holiness " (1 Cor. vii. 14) will surely light up the home of the Christian family with still more heavenly brightness.

The paling stars of the Jewish firmament are about to disappear before the effulgence of the Christian sun of righteousness.

Postponing the consideration of the birth of the holy child Jesus, and its attendant joy, for a subsequent chapter, we may recall the glad emotion which stirred the Jewish breast on the occasion of the Baptist's birth.   The angel announces to Zacharias : " Fear not, Zacharias ;   because thy supplication is heard, and thy wife, Elizabeth, shall bear thee a son, and thou shalt call his name John."   We mark the felicitation of the angel : " *Thou shalt have joy and gladness, and many shall rejoice at his birth.*"   And when to Elizabeth the babe was born, " her neighbours and kinsfolk heard that the Lord had magnified his mercy towards her, and they rejoiced with her."   Then follows the song of praise of Zacharias (Luke i.).

The Apostle Paul recognizes God's goodness as much in his first as in his second birth : " He separated me from my mother's womb, and called me by his grace."

What could possibly be stranger, with a far fainter disclosure of the Fatherhood of God, in pre-Christian times, than for children, esteemed so great a gift, who in Christian times are discovered to be the hideous little monsters the Church paints them ?

Of children then we get a joyous key-note,—a note full of good and of hope for the future, in the New Testament; and above all from the great Teacher Himself ;—a key-note to which we may expect all subsequent teaching in the Christian Church to be attuned.

Let us see what the teaching and practice with regard to children is from the writings of the Fathers,— the *Fathers*, to wit—and ecclesiastical practices, forming or reflecting the general conception of Childhood, in the Christian Church.

Now, although Children find an honoured place in our Christian homes, nothing can be clearer than this: that the theory of unbaptized childhood is as gloomy and as terrible a thing as can well be imagined. So far from being up to the level of Jewish conception, it even sinks below the idea of some of the heathen nations, whose sweet appreciation of Childhood has been illustrated in preceding sections of this work.

As if to enhance the glory of our Father in heaven, it were the most pious thing possible to endow the new-born babe with the attributes of the devil. As if to exalt Him who took little unbaptized children in His arms, it could best magnify the riches of His grace to regard them as little incarnations of evil. As if to honour the work of the Holy Spirit, it were the justest conception that the babes are naturally the objects of divine wrath and displeasure and candidates for an eternity of torture, with perhaps a bare possibility of escape in the uncovenanted mercies of God.

Possibly, the Christian Church, in its zeal for its theological system, has never thought that there may be parents living among us, who, accepting the frightfully depreciatory theory of Childhood, as taught by the Churches, find sanction for the cruel treatment of their offspring, such as the newspapers are almost daily bringing to light in our midst: their own abandoned lives,—with all the sweetness of natural affection obliterated from their characters, looking very like a living testimony to the Church's doctrine of incarnate evil. This is the compliment we pay to our children! We drag these fresh, sparkling embodiments of new life down to our own level of deadness. On the canvas of childhood, after conflicts and often defeats with the powers of evil, we project our own mired humanity, besmirched with the defilements of sin and corruption, and take the children to the font to be washed! And *thus* the fathers have eaten sour grapes and the children's teeth are set on edge (Jer. xxxi. 29). No wonder while "the young men bare the mill, the children stumbled under the wood"! (Lam. v. 13). A little child brought up on the doctrine of original sin,—being assured of a fault by his father, shrewdly retorted: "Well, it was not my fault: it was Adam and Eve's fault"! Was not this artificial feeding?

It is difficult to repress the most scathing language of denunciation of a system which not merely obscures, but which misrepresents the Divine wisdom and benignity, and which has not seldom led a despairing mother to destroy her child.

What has the Christian Church, in almost every section, maintained, as to the nature and the destiny of little children,—even of babes? The fact is too well known. Let us take a glance at the early testimony of the great leaders in Christian Theology and practice, touching Infancy, as brought under notice by

Tracts for the Times—the outcome and stimulus of the " catholic revival" during the last half century.

Tract lxvii., *Ad Clerum.* " Our life is, throughout, represented as commencing, when we are by baptism made members of Christ and children of God : that life may, through our negligence, afterwards decay, or be choked, or smothered, or well-nigh extinguished, and by God's mercy be again renewed and refreshed, but a commencement of spiritual life after Baptism, a death unto sin and a new birth unto righteousness, at any other period than that one first introduction into God's covenant, is as little consonant with the general representations of Holy Scripture, as a commencement of physical life long after our natural birth is with the order of His holy providence."

" One may, indeed, rightly infer that, since the Jews regarded the *baptised* proselyte as a new-born child, our Saviour would not have connected the mention of water with the new birth, unless the new birth which He bestowed, had been bestowed through Baptism : but who would so fetter down the fulness of our Saviour's promises, as that His words should mean nothing more than they would in the mouth of the dry and unspiritual Jewish legalists ? or because they, proud of the covenant with Abraham, deemed that the passing of a proselyte into the outward covenant with Abraham, was a new custom, who would infer that our Saviour only spoke of an *outward* change ? Even some among the Jews had higher notions, and believed that a new soul descended from the region of spirits, upon the admitted proselyte."

The writer afterwards quotes the testimony of *St. Augustine* in the same sense.

" 'Most excellently,' saith he, writing against the Pelagians 'do the Punic Christians entitle Baptism itself no other than salvation, and the sacrament of the body of Christ no other than life.' "*

"Baptism is not a *mere* initiatory rite, but an appointed means for conveying the Holy Spirit."†

Alluding to the Apostle Paul's conversion, the same writer says: "By baptism he was filled with the Holy Ghost." Not pardoned or regenerated till he was baptized.

In a letter to St. Jerome, St. Augustine writes: "Whoever should affirm that infants which die without partaking of this sacrament shall be quickened in Christ, would both go against the Apostle's preaching and also would condemn the whole church (*universam ecclesiam*) . . . . . I do not say that infants dying without the baptism of Christ will be punished with so great pain, so that it were better for them not to have been born, since our Lord spoke this, not of all sinners but of the most profligate and impious ones. . . . . There is no middle place where you can put infants . . . . so that when you confess the infant will not be in the Kingdom, you must acknowledge that he will be in everlasting fire."‡

* *Ad Clerum*, p. 21.   † *Ibid.*, p. 37.
‡ *Epist.* 77 *ad Hieronem de Sancto Victore*, pp. 300-1.

This somewhat confused and illogical statement is marvellous as an exposition of the teaching of Jesus.*

Theodoret is quoted with approval. "'Forgive us our trespasses,' this prayer we do not teach the unconsecrated but the consecrated (baptized) for no unconsecrated person can dare to say '*Our Father*' not having yet received the gift of adoption. But he who has obtained the gift of Baptism calls God 'Father,' as being accounted among the sons of grace."†

St. Gregory of Nazianzum: "Hast thou an infant? ..... Let it be sanctified from a babe. Let it be hallowed by the Spirit from its tenderest infancy. Fearest thou the seal of faith on account of the weakness of the nature, as a faint-hearted mother and of little faith? But Hannah devoted Samuel to God, yea before he was born, and when he was born, immediately made him a priest...... Thou hast no need of amulets, *impart to him the Trinity*, that great and excellent preservative."‡

---

* "This 'washing of the water' was now deemed absolutely necessary for salvation. No human being could pass into the presence of God hereafter, unless he had passed through the waters of baptism here ..... The Pelagian controversy drew out the mournful doctrine, that infants, dying before baptism .... were consigned to everlasting fire. At the close of the fifth century this belief had become universal, chiefly through the means of Augustine..... As to the views of individual Fathers from the time of Augustine it seems impossible to dispute the judgment of the great English authority Wall *On Baptism*: 'How hardsoever this opinion may seem, it is the constant opinion of the Ancients.'"—*Christian Institutions*, by A. P. Stanley, D.D., 4th Edit., 1884.

+ *Ad Clerum*, p. 65.　　‡ *Ibid.*, p. 178.

St. Ambrose : " In baptism there is one thing done
visibly to the eye ; another thing is wrought invisibly
to the mind."

St. Basil : In baptism—"the kingdom of heaven is
there set open."

Chrysostom : " God Himself in baptism, by His in-
visible power halloweth thy head."

St. Gregory of Nyssa : " Baptism, then, is the purifi-
cation of sins, remission of offences, the cause of
regeneration and renewal."

That the amazing operation in Baptism should not
fail of its efficacy, all that appertains to the observance
of the rite must be minutely attended to. The water
must not be ordinary water even though it were double
distilled.

Cyprian tells us that " it is proper the water be
cleansed and sanctified by the priest that it may have
the power in baptism to wash away the sins of him
who is baptized."

And the *Council of Carthage* decrees : " The water
when sanctified by the prayer of the priest washes
away sins."

St. Ambrose says : " The water hath the grace of
Christ ; in it is the presence of the Trinity."

Even so early a writer as Tertullian says : " The
Holy Ghost cometh down and halloweth the water."

In the present book of Common Prayer we have an
authoritative exposition of the doctrine of Baptism.
Though so familiar, its importance, as bearing on the

doctrine of childhood, must excuse so lengthy a quotation from its pages.

" Dearly beloved, forasmuch as all men are conceived and born in sin; and that our Saviour Christ
saith, None can enter into the Kingdom of God, except
he be regenerate and born anew of Water and of the
holy Ghost ; " &c.

What our Lord, the founder of the Christian Church,
said, was, *not* that children were conceived and born in
sin, but that except His adult hearers became once
again. little children they could not enter into the
kingdom of heaven, to which little children, as such,
belonged.   To be born again must be of necessity to
become little children again.   How can little children,
by any process whatever, *become* what they are already ?
Baptism in their case is simply an anachronism.*

---

* It is not forgotten that there is a penitential psalm, written probably by David himself after his guilt had been brought home to him by
Nathan (Ps. li.)   The psalm is not a theological exposition of human
nature at all.   Its inspiration comes from the depths of a passionate
soul, and from an intense consciousness of startling personal moral
delinquency.   It is the heart-broken utterance of a mind prostrate
before the immediate holiness with the black shadow of guilt burdening
the stricken conscience.   David excuses not himself, when, in the
excess of his shame and overwhelming grief, he exclaims : " *Behold, I
was shapen in iniquity ; and in sin did my mother conceive me.*"   Much
less was he deliberately explaining the source and history of his crime,
and still less the melancholy genesis of sin in our world.   Reason failed
him : he had sinned against reason.   Language failed him : words
could not express the heinousness of his offence before God : explanation of himself to himself seemed impossible.   Have we not become

In the first prayer, we are reminded of the sanctification of water to the mystical washing away of sin, and the deliverance of the child from God's wrath, the child—of whom Jesus said "of such is the kingdom of heaven"!

And then, without perceiving the glaring contradiction, the Gospel is read, the Gospel in which these very children of God's wrath are, we find, models of the kingdom of heaven, and as such, are taken up in the arms of the Holy Jesus and blessed.

Then comes a ministerial exhortation, in which (and before the administration of the rite too!) the child's *innocency* is declared and held up for imitation.

This is followed by an address to the godfathers and godmothers, in which they are reminded that they

painfully familiar with the exclamation of one who has fallen into sin, "I can't think how I came to do it!" And in David's anguish we have a mirror in which all have seen themselves whose spiritual sensitiveness has been deeply stirred in view of their own grievous departure from the perfect standard of divine holiness. The greatest saints have been the most profoundly affected by "the exceeding sinfulness of sin." There is doubtless a great deal of truth in the doctrine of hereditary taint, and it is ignored neither in the Old nor New Testament. But a generalization from the fervid expression of a mind almost shattered with a sense of sin, and to accept as God's deliberate utterance the cry of human weakness and remorse, is a remarkable illustration of the blind spirit of Theology. In this instance, as in many other cases, the truth of Holy Writ is verifiable in our own experience or observation. The story is *so* true! And yet upon this Psalm one of the most frightful dogmas of the Theology of the Christian Church mainly rests.

have been praying that the young innocent child may be released from his sins, &c.,

After the baptism the Priest shall say: " Seeing now, dearly beloved brethren, that this Child is regenerate," &c., And then the prayer following: "We yield Thee hearty thanks, most merciful Father, that it hath pleased Thee to regenerate this Infant," &c.,

The concluding paragraph is also worthy of notice : " It is certain by God's Word, that Children which are baptized, dying before they commit actual sin, are undoubtedly saved."

Can anyone draw the inevitable conclusion from this doctrine of the Church of England, without a shudder of horror ?

The writer of the Oxford Tract, to which reference has already been made says, with regard to the second Prayer Book of Edward VI., "some things were omitted, which, if retained, had been a blessing to us ; but all our Service which remained, came from the pure sources of Christian Antiquity." What were some of these things ?—and as the Oxford movement is still developing in the English Church, is there not some hope in the hearts of our priests of securing a restoration of the good things omitted in the present Service ?

Then we may yet see the water exorcised and the devils cast out of the infants. For thus the priest, looking upon the little child, was taught to say: " I command thee, unclean spirit, in the name of the

Father, of the Son, and of the Holy Ghost, that thou come out, and depart from these infants whom our Lord Jesus Christ hath vouchsafed to call to His holy baptism, to be made members of His body, and of His holy congregation. Therefore, thou cursed spirit, remember thy sentence, remember thy judgment, remember the day to be at hand wherein thou shalt burn in fire everlasting, prepared for thee and thy angels. And presume not hereafter to exercise any tyranny towards these infants, whom Christ hath bought with His precious blood, and by this, His holy baptism, calleth to be of His flock."

There is no exorcism in the present baptismal service, but the stipulation of the sponsors is that the child shall renounce the devil and all his works.

The consecration and exorcism of the water of baptism formed an important part of the baptismal ceremony.

But we have not quite done with the water yet. According to our Tractarian friend, " it was believed that the element of water at the creation, by the Spirit of God moving upon it, received a peculiar and specific virtue, by which it was especially fitted and appointed to cleanse and sanctify the soul."

But even this does not seem to have been thought enough, for the doctrine of the Fathers is, that our Lord submitted to baptism, that He might sanctify water to the washing away of sin, and impart to it the power of cleansing the soul.

But this double sanctification is not enough. The water must be exorcised, and then it must be consecrated, and we have the prayer: "Sanctify this water to the mystical washing away of *sin*."

Still something more wonderful from the annals of Church History. Gregory Nazianzen, Basil, Prosper and Jerome, and many others maintain the presence of Christ's blood in the water after consecration. With as good reason " it might be affirmed that the consecrated water is red as it moves in the blessed font of immortality. Why not say with Isidore, that it is really the water that flowed from the side of Christ?"*

Where stop at absurdities? Why not believe with Leo, the Pontiff, that a man after baptism is not the same as he was before, but the body being regenerated *becomes* the flesh of Him who was crucified?†

We get a reminiscence of Leo in the poetry of the *Christian Year*, but it seems to be more than poetry as quoted by Rev. Dr. Pusey.

> " What sparkles in that lucid flood
> Is water by gross mortals eyed,
> But seen by faith 'tis blood
> Out of a dear friend's side.‡

It is only fair to the earliest writers on Christian doctrine, to remember that absolute silence about

---

* *Vide* Halley *On the Sacraments*, p. 221.

† Leo, *Serm.* 14, *De Passione.*

‡ In answer to the question "What is faith ? " to a class of Sunday School boys; the answer of a genius was " Believing what isn't true, teacher."

N

baptismal regeneration prevails.   Clement of Rome,
Ignatius, and Polycarp are silent.   No trace of it can
be found before Justin Martyr's *First Apology, circa*
A.D. 140 or 150. As a gathering cloud, from that
date to the time of Clement of Alexandria and
Tertullian, the doctrine began to spread itself over the
Christian Church.

The baptism of infants was unknown to the apostolic churches.   In patristic times children were only
recognized as God's children after Baptism.   Dug out
of the quarry of humanity, and chiselled by the ecclesiastical sculptors, a little child was henceforth en-
dowed with the right to say, " Abba, Father."   The
logical deduction was that none but these could say
the Lord's prayer : nay, the catechumens were strictly
forbidden to be present when it was repeated.   " From
that service, as Chrysostom calls it, all the unbaptized
were most scrupulously and rigorously excluded."*

In the Baptismal Service of the English Church we
find words from the Gospel of St. Mark thrust into
the midst of the service, which are strikingly opposed

---

* Referring to Wordsworth and Keble, Dean Stanley writes : " It is
instructive to observe that whilst the sentiments of the two poets on the
natural attractiveness of children are identical, Keble often endeavours
to force it into a connection with Baptism which to Wordsworth is
almost unknown.   It is said that Wordsworth, once reading with
admiration a well-known poem in the *Christian Year*, stumbled at the
opening line, ' Where is it mothers learn their love ? ' (to which the
answer is ' The Font').   ' No, no,' said the old poet, ' it is from their own
maternal hearts.' " *Christian Institutions*, 1884, p. 32.

to the Church doctrine in which they are imbedded, and which are there as a standing protest against the whole proceeding.

" The Sacramental principle had been most plainly adopted by our Lord ; the spiritual forces with which He would renew the face of the earth, were to be excited through material instruments ; and He Himself had secured the principle from uncertainty or vagueness or individualism in its expression by appointing, with the utmost weight and penetration of His authority, the definite form of two great ordinances, which were to begin to advance the supernatural life of His members, to extend the range of His church, and to maintain its unity. . . . To be living a life received, nourished and characterised by Baptism and by the Eucharist —this is the distinctive note of a Christian—thus does he differ from other men. The Sacrament by which he became a member of Christ's body must determine throughout the two distinctive qualities of his inner life."*

Why good Christian men of the second, third, fourth and fifth centuries of the Christian Era, should be held responsible for the life, thought and functions of all Christians to the end of time, seems more than their successors have any right to impose upon them. Personal responsibility cannot be shifted from the individual to any number of saintly men, however

* Rev. F. Paget, D.D., Professor of Pastoral Theology, *On the Sacraments*, p. 420.

comfortable it might be thought (as in the case of Cardinal Newman) to be relieved of it.

Christians are waking up to the fact. The truth is that the Fathers had the misfortune, without knowing it, to shift the ground of the Christian life and society from its true spiritual basis to an intellectual foundation.

Propositions led to controversy. That was voted true which majorities affirmed. Authority made its demands and anathema fenced authority with its fearful imprecations. The subject of the Infinite was *defined (!)* in the Trinitarian formulary of Athanasius, whatever the poor pretensions or disavowals to metaphysical subtlety of objectors might be. There is all the difference between love and logic! The love of Christ constrains and unites. Logical propositions do not touch the sentiments and affections of the soul. From systems of theology, multitudes are finding their way out of the mazes of dogma, to the personal living Christ.

We have thus far confined our inquiry on the subject of Infant Baptism especially to the Church Fathers, and their English successors, the Oxford Tractarians, of half a century ago; half a century is more than the average of human life. It might be argued that it is hardly fair to make the Christianity of the present day responsible for the theology and practice of former times. With the progress of clearer perceptions of the Divine Fatherhood, whether in the Church or outside it, our views concerning the nature of childhood and its relation to God as revealed in Christ Jesus have been advanced by the modern investigations of physiologists, psychologists, educationists, and evolutionists.

It is satisfactory, so far as the English Church is concerned, to find that the water, in which a babe is baptized, is pure enough without being exorcised, that there is no supernatural impediment in actual demoniacal possession by evil spirits to the child's baptism.

The Presbyterian Church is not very clear on the subject of Infant Baptism, though its Confession of Faith could hardly be used to cover the doctrines and practice of the English Church.

The baptism of the Presbyterians is " not absolutely to regeneration and salvation," " nor are all that are baptized undoubtedly regenerated." It is required that one or both parents of the child presented for baptism be a believer.

" Grace is not only offered but *really bestowed* (whether to those of age or infants) as that grace belongeth unto, according to the counsel of God's own will in His appointed time." It thus appears, that, on compliance with the conditions named, the baptized infant enjoys some privilege, though on the occasion of the baptism the appointed time for its actual bestowal may be future.

The *value* of the child's reception into " the bosom of the visible church," to be taught to the congregation must depend entirely upon the meaning attached to the term—visible church. But in the instructions to ministers as to the subjects to be made prominent at the child's baptism, they are to understand that the baptized child is now entered into *the household of faith*.

Sacramentarians may find a great deal of support in the Westminster Confession; may we not say that the Presbyterians are not so very distantly related to them, after all?

Thus we have got in direct statement and still more by implication, an idea of what childhood in the Christian Church is. "Original sin," and the possibility of "a double dose of it," has even found its way into the British House of Commons, by the mouth of the most eminent British Statesman of our times. Baptismal regeneration has been generally abandoned by the Reformed and Protestant Churches, but with rare exceptions, the child of Christendom has been unreservedly endowed by birth with the repulsive features of Augustine whether we follow him in the Dutch Presbyterian, the Scotch Presbyterian* or the Congregational schools of our country. And in the words of "the Shorter Catechism of the Westminster Assembly of Divines,"—"All mankind, by the fall, lost communion with God, are under His wrath and curse,

* "By the decree of God, for the manifestation of His glory (!) some men and angels are predestinated unto everlasting life and others fore-ordained to everlasting death." Presbyterian *Confession of Faith.*

and so made liable to all the miseries of this life, to death itself, and the pains of hell for ever." Imagination may depict the mournful procession of little children! Mark their little tripping footsteps, for in their ignorance they are as light-hearted as can be imagined. There they go! little scape-graces of Rome: *enfants terribles* of the English Church; monstrosities of the American Dutch Reformed Church;* broods of young serpents of Scotch Calvinism; and bringing up the rear—last and least—Calvin's own non-elect babes on their way to hell, where, according to his measurement, they may be found a span long. But—stop the procession, for after all, it is only a tragedy of theological romance; and, baptism or no baptism, our practical humanity, truly Christian in its moral strength and tender affections, is full of the most beautiful specimens of family life. We may join in the old Psalmist's exultant delight: "Happy is the man that hath his quiver full of them."

Baxter shows how Presbyterianism theologizes:—

"None ought to be baptized but those that either personally deliver up themselves in covenant to God the Father, Son, and Holy Ghost, professing a true repentance and faith, and consent to the covenant; or else are thus delivered up, and dedicated, and entered into covenant in their infancy, by those that being Christians themselves, have so much interest in them and power of them, that their act may be esteemed

* "Conceived and born in sin, and therefore children of wrath."

as the infant's act, and legally imputed to them as if
themselves had done it."*

"*Q.:* Are any children guilty of their parents' sins?

"*A.:* Yes; all children are *guilty* of the sins which
their parents committed before their birth, while they
were in their loins. Not with the same degree and
sort of guilt as the parents are, but yet with so much
as exposeth them to *just penalties.*

" *Q.:* How prove you that?

" *A.:* First by the nature of the case; for though
we were not personally existent in them when they
sinned, we were seminally existent in them, which is
more than causally or virtually; and it was that semen
which was guilty in them, that was after made a
person, and so that person must have the same guilt."†

In so far as it bears on the question of heredity the
following question and answer gives a somewhat hopeful view of the tendency of the evil virus to vanish from
the race.

"*Q.:* Why doth God name only the third and fourth
generation?

"*A.:* To show us, that though He will punish the
sins of His enemies on their posterity who imitate their
parents, yet He sets such bounds to the execution of
His justice, as that sinners shall not want encouragement to repent and hope for mercy."‡

" It is the will of God that infants be members of
the Christian church, of which baptism is the entrance.

* Baxter's *Works*, vol. v., p. 46.   † Vol. xix., p. 176.   ‡ Vol. xix., p. 177.

For there is no proof that ever God had a church on earth in any age, of which infants were not members."*

"*Q.:* What the better are infants for being baptized ?

"*A.:* The children of the faithful are stated by it in a right to the aforesaid benefits of the covenant, the pardon of their original sin, the love of God, the intercession of Christ, and the help of the Holy Ghost, when they come to age, and title to the Kingdom of .Heaven, if they die before they forfeit it."†

* Vol. xix., p. 264.
† The whole of the above from Rd. Baxter's *Works.*

CHAPTER VIII.

THE VOICE OF THE PROFESSING CHURCH THROUGH ITS CHILDREN'S HYMNS.

THE child of the Christian institutions can hardly be expected to escape the influence of the Church's theology in its religious training.

Through its catechisms it is taught to say things it cannot believe to be true; to confess to sins it has never committed; and to sing songs that, if realised as fact, would crush its little heart.

And, awful though it be to think of mocking God in forms of worship, it is a comfort to believe that the " thoughtless tongue " of a child is its salvation from impiety towards the Divine Father while it is its protection against its own misery.

As truer and more Christ-like conceptions of the great Father have been adopted in recent times, by nearly all the Christian communities, the grosser, harsher, crueller representations of God have receded into the dark ages, and the many charming hymns and songs of modern writers, at once spiritual and poetical, have been sweetly attuned to the chords of grace and love struck by the Christ Himself.

But even in the present day the vestiges of a patristic

and mediæval theology float upon the melodies which little children are taught from the cradle to sing. .

Episcopalians, Presbyterians and Nonconforming bodies are forward in *in*doctrinating their children through the medium of their "Divine songs" with the theology of their respective churches.

The Baptism of our English Church, as the cause or even as the sign only of a baby's second birth, implies a condition of sin which is washed away in the administration of the baptismal rite.

Mrs. Alexander stands deservedly high as a writer of "hymns for children," but the hymn on "Holy Baptism" is not such a hymn as the Christ would regard as a happy expression of His mind touching the unbaptized little child that He held up as a pattern to the disciples, when He said, "of such is the Kingdom of Heaven."

Thus the children are taught by Mrs. Alexander to sing :—

> "In the name of God the Father,
>   Of the Son and Holy Ghost,
> He* baptized us then and made us
>   Soldiers in our Master's host."

Again, hymn 72 :—

> "We were washed in holy water,
>   We were set Christ's Church within,
> Gifted with His Holy Spirit,
>   And forgiven all our sin."

There are other hymns by this gifted composer

. * The priest.

through which the same sacramental grace is trace-able.

Another child's hymnal of extensive circulation, called *The Praises of Jesus, a Hymn Book for Children,* contains the following :—

> " The pure baptismal wave
>   Hath washed its sin away;
> Unhindered, it may pass
>   To glad eternal day "

implying that the little innocent but unbaptized babe is doomed to eternal night.

On the same lines in *Hymns Ancient and Modern,* we learn that,

> Within the Church's sacred fold,
> By holy sacrament enroll'd
>   Another lamb we lay:
> An heir before of sin and shame,
> Now in the Holy Triune name
>   His guilt is washed away.
>
> *   *   *   *
>
> O loving Father, Thee we pray
> Look on this babe new-born to-day.
>
> *   *   *   *

The following verses are from the *People's Hymnal.*

> Begotten at the font
>   By God the Spirit's power
> A gentle lamb from Satan snatched
>   In childhood's helpless hour.
>
> And all the host of heaven
>   Rejoice before the Lord,
> To see one child of fallen man,
>   A child of God restored.

> Lord, to-day, we bring to Thee,
>   With a cleansed and perfect soul,
> This, Thy little one to be,
>   Entered on Thy muster roll.

Other hymns there are which teach the children that there could not be a more wretched world to be born into than this. Its parents must be vile,—the stream cannot be better than the fountain,—and the only gleam of hope for the little one comes from an infinitely remote heaven, to which it may go some day, and the sooner the better.

> " There is a happy land
>   Far, far away."

Again Dr. Watts puts into the mouths of little children to sing;

> " There is a dreadful hell,
>   And everlasting pains,
> Where sinners must with devils dwell
>   In darkness, fire and chains.
>
> Can such a wretch as I
>   Escape this cursed end ?
> And may I hope whene'er I die
>   I shall to heaven ascend ?
>
> Then will I read and pray,
>   While I have life and breath,
> Lest I should be cut off to-day
>   And sent to eternal death."

So they are taught to sing, " I want to be an angel," though they are occasionally reminded that the devil has *his* angels too.

The result of it all is most depressing to the child's
tender spirit, and utterly confusing to the child's
enquiring mind.

A Nonconformist minister has written a Boy's
Hymn—a recoil from the angel type of hymn, which is
like a breath of fresh air on coming out of an ill-venti-
lated church. It is headed, " A Boy's Hymn : "*

> I want to live to be a man
> Both good and useful all I can,
> To speak the truth, be just and brave,
> My fellow men to help and save.
>
> I want to live that I may show
> My love to Jesus here below ;
> In human toil to take my share
> And thus for angel's work prepare.

The modern character of Hymnody in sweetness
and purity and spiritual grace from a hard, theological
form of doctrine, marks the progress of the Church
of Christ towards the life and action of Apostolic
times.

The catechisms will stand or fall with the creeds
and liturgies of the churches.

* Rev. Newman Hall.

CHAPTER IX.

THE UNIT OF THE KINGDOM OF HEAVEN—A LITTLE CHILD.

"And they brought unto him little children, that he should touch them: and the disciples rebuked them. But when Jesus saw it, he was moved with indignation, and said unto them, Suffer the little children to come unto me; forbid them not: for of such is the kingdom of God. Verily I say unto you, Whosoever shall not receive the kingdom of God as a little child, he shall in no wise enter therein. And he took them in his arms, and blessed them, laying his hands upon them."—MARK x. 13—16.

"And they came to Capernaum: and when he was in the house he asked them, What were ye reasoning in the way? But they held their peace: for they had disputed one with another in the way, who was the greatest. And he sat down, and called the twelve; and he saith unto them, If any man would be first, he shall be last of all, and minister of all. And he took a little child, and set him in the midst of them: and taking him in his arms, he said unto them, Whosoever shall receive one of such little children in my name, receiveth me: and whosoever receiveth me, receiveth not me, but him that sent me."—MARK ix. 33—37.

How refreshing to escape from the stuffy schoolroom of a heartless Theology, into the free, inspiring air of the presence of the great Teacher, under Heaven's blue sky and by the side of the Lake of Galilee!

It is quite true. Jesus is about to found a Kingdom.

What do men do who propose to raise an institution, to start a company, to establish a dynasty?

According to modern notions, the enterprise must be manned by the most influential names that can be brought together; the magnetism of money must attract, and an influential ministry or directorate must be formed. The widest possible foundation must be laid, and the broader the base the more imposing the superstructure.

What was our Lord's method? Nobody would ever guess it. It was a method that was never dreamt of in anybody's philosophy. It was the very inversion of the *plan* devised by the shrewdest scheming. Jesus began not with the philosophical or clever base, but with the apex—a little child!

But, it may be said, "No, Jesus began by calling twelve men,—and with *these* He began the development of His Kingdom."

Granted: but, for all that, we have in these twelve men, the almost undefiled elements of childhood; and, still more strikingly we have the absence of those qualifications which are considered absolutely necessary for the launching of any merely human enterprise.

1. The fishermen were poor. Children have no money. They come into the world without pockets. Pockets for children are often a retrograde step. Pockets lead to the discovery that all *things are not theirs*. To the veritable child Paul truly says: "All things are yours." The covetous spirit is often born and bred in a child's pocket. Only think of cramming the world into one's pocket: it is what many are continually attempting.

2. The fishermen were not learned. *Children know nothing.* Their minds have no preoccupations. Paul was a perfect child when he wrote : " I determined not to know anything among you, save "—

3. The twelve were without position or social importance. Children have no idea of superior or inferior. A baby prince and a gutter babe know no distinction. They both have mothers,—that is all, and quite enough for them.

4. The twelve were unfettered. They were not clothed with civil or ecclesiastical authority. They were free to forsake all and follow the Christ.

The most delightful time for a little child is when it is just stripped of its clothes. Then it luxuriates in its sense of freedom. How often has vanity sprung up in the heart of a little girl when it has been put into a smart frock !

Nicodemus had so far parted with the simple qualifications of childhood, that to him, to be born again had become a necessity. And Nicodemus was only a specimen of other masters in Israel.

The rich young man, whose conscious integrity in the keeping of the law, gave him, as he thought, a special claim to the eternal life, forgot that he too had pockets ; but alas, they had become so expanded that there was no getting through the only gate for him, the needle's eye, into the kingdom of heaven.

But the twelve : though in some marked characteristics, like little children, were found wanting. They

o

had not, by any means, escaped the contamination of the worldly spirit. On the contrary, the obscurity, from which they were emerging, had its devious dangers for the childlike spirit. Instead of self-depreciation, self-assertive ambition and the race for precedence began to manifest themselves. If they had left all and followed their Lord, in the first warm appreciation of their impulsive natures; cold calculation supervened, and the question—What shall we *get* by it?—expressed the ambition and covetousness which are not of the kingdom of heaven.

The question was put to the Master. Did the mother of Zebedee's children really mean to steal a march on the claims of other disciples in favour of her two sons? The strife for the mastery—the struggle for priority formed a prominent feature in their lives. How could Jesus cast out this evil spirit? He could cast out devils,—give sight to the blind,—unstop deaf ears, and even raise to life, with a word. He could still the tempest with "a hush." But this demon of premiership?

Again, it may be asked where is the religion or the philosophy that propounds such an antidote for this poison? This devil is not to be exorcised by miraculous interposition. The Revealer has the secret. Jesus took a little child and set him in the midst. An object lesson, as profound as it is simple, is enough for a wise and understanding heart. Our Lord could find nothing more fitting, more beautiful, more attractive, on this earth, than a little child, as an epitome of *greatness* in the Kingdom of Heaven.

Argument seems superfluous in presence of so clear an objective presentation of our Lord's conception of children.

Can the contempt of the immediate disciples of Jesus for children be the germ out of which has sprung the monstrous theories of the Christian Church?

See! the mothers are bringing the children that He might touch them. The disciples are assuming the function of the police. But the mothers press on with the children. What should be allowed to deter them? "The benignity of His countenance invites us," says one tender-hearted mother. Another full of the motherhood of God, says: "He can't refuse us." A third:—"His simple touch has healing in it." A fourth says, "Come along, my boy; I know there must be virtue in the hem of His garment." The disciples may scowl; but the mothers only see Jesus. But on this occasion they are not brought to Jesus for healing: there is not one mother urged by her anxiety that her child might be made whole; much less are they seeking personal help, or some material blessing. They are absorbed in their darling children. Of itself this self-abnegation on the part of the mothers would have made way for the children. They brought them to Jesus that He might simply give them His blessing.

And Jesus took them up in His arms and blessed

them.   The most Christian thing that the Christ
could do !

Could any mother of these little ones have been disappointed that He did not exorcise their offspring, or
baptize them, or ask for their godfathers and godmothers ?

Jesus blessed them.   He took them up in His arms
and pressed them to His tender heart.   The scene has
the beauty and fragrance of Paradise about it.   It was
the outward and visible sign of the atmosphere and
bliss of heaven, where their angels do always behold
the Father's face.

"Women and children" have been in all ages
classed together in a somewhat sinister sense.
Women, especially mothers, and children have
received distinguished honour from the Son of man.
The depreciation of woman is a reproach which
modern Christian civilization has well nigh wiped out.
And in social life the prophecy—"a little child shall
lead them," receives larger fulfilment.

"And Jesus took a little child and set him in the
midst."   The little child is still living, and Jesus is
still saying, "Except ye be converted and become as
this little child ye cannot enter into the kingdom of
heaven."   He is still saying, "Now ye are clean through
the word which I have spoken unto you."   He speaks
the word, and He still points to the illustration.   Has
this been a word of Salvation to *us* ?   Do we believe in
the Christ – and in these sayings of His ?   And have

they been the means of our conversion? Has it not often rather been thought that the child has been committed to our care, that we might convert *it?* What an inversion of the spiritual order! You have got to change places with the child—you greatest ones in the kingdom of heaven—you have to come down from your self-exaltation that you may find the means of your conversion in the little child. *See what you can get out of the child, not what you can cram into it.* And do not say this is one of the extraordinary, out-of-the-way lessons taught by Christ to His disciples under peculiar circumstances. Except ye—ALL ye who want to be more than little children—be converted and become as this little child, there is no way of entrance into the kingdom of heaven for you—for any of you—for any of us in all the world and in all time. There are *only* children in heaven.

With a delicate apprehension of child-nature, Horace Bushnell writes: "When we preach to little children we are not coming down to them, we are rather coming up from the subterranean hells of grown-up sin."

In a speech by Edward White* he tells us "Binney said: 'we ought not to teach children that they require to be converted.' He was fond of pointing out our Lord's example when the apostles had been quarreling, as apostles sometimes will: 'And He took a little child and set him in the midst of them;' and He did not say to the child, 'unless you are converted and

* *Independent*, July 15, 1891.

become like these grown-up people you cannot enter
into the kingdom of heaven,' but He said to the grown-
up people, ' except you are converted and become like
this little child, ye shall not enter into the kingdom of
heaven.' "

John Ruskin has a fine appreciation of childhood.

He points out four leading features :—1. It is
modest. The child does not think it can teach its
parents, or that it knows everything. On the contrary,
it is always asking questions and wanting to know
more. 2. It is *faithful.* Perceiving that its father
knows best what is good for it, gives him its hand,
and will walk blindfold with him, if he bids it. 3. It
is *loving.* Give a little love to a child, and you get
a great deal back. You cannot please it so much
as by giving it a chance of being useful, in ever so
humble a way. And because of all these characters it
is *cheerful.* Putting its trust in its father, it is careful
for nothing—being full of love to every creature, it is
happy always, whether in its play or its duty.

"Humility, Faith, Charity, and Cheerfulness. That's
what you've got to be converted to. ' Except ye be
converted and become as little children,' " ye cannot
enter the Kingdom of Heaven.

"Backsliding, indeed! I can tell you, on the ways
most of us go, the faster we slide back the better. . . .
Back, I tell you; back—out of your long faces, and into
your long clothes. It is among children only, and as
children only, that you will find medicine for your

healing and true wisdom for your teaching.   There is
poison in the counsels of the *men* of this world; the
words they speak are all bitterness, 'the poison of
asps is under their lips,' but 'the sucking child shall
play by the hole of the asp.'   There is death in the
looks of men.   'Their eyes are privily set against the
poor:' they are as the uncharmable serpent, the
cockatrice, which slew by seeing.   But 'the weaned
child shall lay his hand on the cockatrice' den'......
There is death in the thoughts of men: the world is
one wide riddle to them, darker and darker as it draws
to a close; but the secret of it is known to the child,
and the Lord of heaven and earth is most to be
thanked in that 'He has hidden these things from
the wise and prudent, and has revealed them unto
babes'......it is not out of the mouths of the knitted
gun,......but 'out of the mouths of babes and suck-
lings' that the strength is ordained, which shall 'still
the enemy and avenger.'"

A few years ago the writer paid a visit to a house
in one of the busiest thoroughfares in London, doomed
to come down under the fiat of Metropolitan Improvements.   It had been occupied till recently, by a provision merchant, and the shop on the ground floor,
stripped of everything but the counters, egg cases and
shelves, and some large casks, looked gloomy and deso-
late.   But a benevolent lady with warm sympathies for
the little waifs and strays of the London streets, saw
her opportunity, and on the evening of the visit the

desolate-looking shop had been converted into a garden of the Lord, and in this unexpected quarter the desert was actually rejoicing and blossoming as the rose.

For several successive Monday evenings this lady had collected as many boys and girls as liked to come. The counters and egg-boxes had been converted into seats, and every available shelf and cask were occupied by little ones from four to fourteen years of age.

The singing was good and even sweet. Answers to questions were elicited that testified to the intelligent attention of the children to their teacher's address which was anecdotal and impressive.

The discipline and order were remarkable. The severest punishment consisted in temporary exclusion. " My dear boy," said the lady to a lad who was there that night for the first time, " you don't understand our rules. You must go ; but if you will be good, you may come next Monday; " and the disgraced boy walked quietly out in shame, and one could not but perceive in sorrow. Two other boys were dismissed in this way during the evening.

These children were gutter children, coming from the courts and alleys in the immediate neighbourhood of the densely populated district of Seven Dials. Their faces looked clean; their clothes—their best and worst—would hardly have constituted a ticket of admission to our nice respectable Sunday Schools.

What struck the writer was this : these children were growing up under the most unfavourable condi-

tions, physical and moral. Pictures of their surroundings have been given by Mayhew, Sims and others.
They need not be described here. Could anything be
more hopelessly discouraging ?

Swept from the streets into this shop, and packed
closely together, what could be expected to be got out
of this mass of scum ?

And yet, looking at the class of 110 to 120 of such
unpromising children, crowding in eagerly, behaving in
an orderly manner, listening attentively, and falling
into sympathy with the teacher so readily—evidently
enjoying the whole thing as a treat, and this after a
few meetings, only once a week, what will adequately
and fairly explain the phenomenon ?

To the writer's mind it comes with all the force of
demonstration—visible, actual, irrefutable—that below
the surface of neglect, in spite of seeds of evil in their
early growth, "good ground " had been reached. In
these little ones "the kingdom of heaven was at hand,"
and the ground was being cleared.

The children were now, if never before, treated in
harmony with the essential principles of their nature.
The treatment came to them as more truly *natural*,
than the life they were living in the gutter. They
were God's children and they were beginning to
realize the fact, under the Christian tact of their
teacher. They were now breathing the very air they
were born to breathe, and we fancied they looked,
some of them, a little surprised that they could breathe

it so freely. The light—quite a surprising light in the midst of *their* darkness—that now shone upon them, was just the light for which their large, wondering eyes were formed. They were of the kingdom of heaven by birth, and they found themselves entering into the enjoyment of their birthright.

Few of them, probably, had grasped the idea of fatherhood through their earthly parent, and possibly the divine Fatherhood now being revealed to them would come upon them with all the strangeness of a surprise. But each boy and girl was a child, and the Father is the complement of the child. The children found themselves at home in this old shop.

Our blessed Lord was ever true to the child—the type of the kingdom of heaven, and after the resurrection He saluted His disciples as children.

Manifesting Himself to them at the lake of Tiberias, at the break of day, Jesus stood on the beach, and called to the disciples, who had toiled all the night and caught nothing. The disciple who was of the most childlike spirit, was the first to identify the Master, and he woke up Peter to the fact—" It is the Lord." Our Lord asked them, "*Children*, have ye aught to eat ? " A very little time had elapsed since the child-lesson had been given to them, and the intense realization of the presence of their Lord must have dissipated from their hearts the petty ambitions which had disturbed their peace.

The Apostle, who called himself " less than the

least," frequently alludes to childhood as carrying with it special advantages. ("Children and heirs," Rom. viii. 17). And in exhorting the Ephesian Christians: " Be ye therefore followers of God, as dear children ; " Eph. v. 1; "Walk as children of light : " Eph. v. 8.

Peter exhorts—"as children of obedience, not fashioning yourselves according to your former lusts in the time of your ignorance;" and he prefaces the exhortation with "be sober, and set your hope perfectly on the grace that is being brought unto you at the revelation of Jesus Christ;" suggesting emphatically that the revelation of *the Son*, is the hope and blessedness of true childhood.

And John, of the child-spirit especially, in tender sympathy writes: "my little children;" "ye are of God, little children ;" and declares that he has "no greater joy than to see his children walking in the truth."

Thus was the type of the Master perpetuated, and illustrated in the writings of His followers.

An allusion is all that is here necessary to the holy child Jesus. He was the perfect and beloved Son of God—the first-born of every creature. Every lesson He taught was exemplified in His own true life. There is no need to draw upon the apocryphal stories which tradition records. All that He claimed as essential to a child, characterised His own conduct; and it is only as we grow up with Him in all things, that the true image of a little child reveals itself.

CHAPTER X.

THE CHILD AS PORTRAYED BY JESUS.

" Of such is the Kingdom of Heaven."

CHURCH dogmas, as we have seen, in theory and practice, could not present to our Lord a child that should at all answer the Master's description, or serve as the specimen to be held up as representative of His Kingdom before His disciples.

But our Lord did not wait until the churches had decided the question of childhood many centuries after He had left the earth. He could trust the children with the evidence they bore in their constitution as to their nature ; and whether before or subsequently to baptism, they were of His Kingdom just the same.

Let us carefully recall the Kingdom of Heaven as defined by the great Teacher. It is not meat and drink, but righteousness and peace and joy in the Holy Spirit. It is spiritual in its righteous peace and joy. It is not an institution at all, it is a condition of heart, and soul, and life. Its essential characteristics are *love, faith, hope,* as described by St. Paul in 1 Cor. xiii.

These are not the qualities which were displayed by

the disciples when they held a council on the road, without waiting to vote anyone to the chair; not much of the righteousness, or joy, or peace of the kingdom of heaven did they manifest. Faith, hope, charity—these three—were simply inverted and concentrated on self and not on their Master. They were near Him, but just then a long way from the kingdom in which they were clamouring to be pre-eminent.

The little child Jesus took up was not only much nearer, but was actually of the Kingdom of Heaven itself.

We must leave the theologians to settle their difference with the Friend of the children, and proceed to enquire *how* are little children of the Kingdom of Heaven ?

All will agree with the writer that faith, hope, and love are essential attributes of the Christian. Why should we not agree that these qualities inhere in every child that is born in a healthy condition ? These qualities incipiently characterize every babe that is born into our world.

A natural mother loves her babe—the babe instinctively loves the mother. The babe *trusts* the parent, as the natural father challenges the confidence of the child. And hope, springing perennial in the human breast, is inspired by the mutual love and faith of both parent and child.

Developing intelligence under human, kindly influences, will tend to expand and strengthen these beautiful, divine attributes, and the child will grow in favour with God and man.

Unfortunately the Christian church almost universally, has philosophised on these essential facts of life, till these charming qualities of our true humanity are dissected with the theological knife, hung up on Church Articles, and the child is passed through the mysterious processes which result in its being something *less* than when it came fresh from Heaven.

Is there any truer, better, more real sense in which children can be held up to men—to disciples even—as samples of the kingdom of Heaven ?   How, indeed, are our Lord's words to be held in any way as true, besides this ?

That they are true, we can at any time verify for ourselves.

Take a little child, and take a man who has had some experience of human life.   Cannot you feel sure at once of the vocal response of a little child to your sympathetic approach to it?   The child has an *openness* which expresses its faith—is pleased as you touch its affection, and as the wonder of hopeful expectation is awakened.

On the other hand, the man of experience knows enough to be hesitant, doubting, uncertain—even suspicious; he will not wear his heart upon his sleeve before his fellow men.   It cannot be helped in this social imperfect evil state.   But who does not envy the little one who is, as yet, uncorrupted by the world, and needs no regeneration?

We take for consideration these three divine virtues. They are attributes of a human soul as yet uncorrupted by bad education or example.

We take them as St. Paul took them. No Bible reader is more familiar with any passage in the Book than that portion of his first epistle to the Corinthians, in which he discourses on the nature and action of love. He discusses "charity" as what it is or what it is not, and as it comports itself under every variety of circumstance. It is not a theological essay, but an analysis of the most beautiful phenomenon in the universe—in its highest, purest and sweetest form.

It comes from the heart of God; it was embodied in Christ Jesus; and it never faileth, as it comes to us in a little child.

Again, we have *faith*, in the eleventh chapter of the Epistle to the Hebrews, treated in the same philosophical spirit. But instead of being analyzed as love is, by St. Paul in 1 Cor., we have it illustrated in human life and character. The principle of *faith* is the same whether we detect it in Rahab and Samson, or in St. Paul and St. Peter.

Both *love* and *faith* are brought under our notice by these writers, quite apart from any theological system, whether of High Church, Broad Church, or Low Church, or no church at all. These are essential to the humanity of which Jesus is the head.*

* " The head of every man is Christ."—1 Cor. xi. 3.

And these qualities of the soul, apart from educational influences, are to be found as Jesus found them
—in little children ; and it is simply on this broad
ground that children are claimed by Jesus as of the
kingdom of heaven.

CHAPTER XI.

CONCLUSION.

THAT the child is essentially the same in all ages, is an affirmation in perfect harmony with the analogy of nature. The ascent and song of the lark under the canopy of heaven is the same now as it has ever been.

Man is the only animal that can live under every variety of climate ; and although his nature may undergo modifications due to climatic variation and mode of existence, he is essentially the same in the constitution of his nature.

He develops according to the *Civilization* in which he is reared, but the broad outlines of his nature remain.

The colour of his skin may suggest his geographical relations. His dress may tell of his political and social surroundings. His occupations and habits may indicate his mental calibre and his means of living. But notwithstanding all the circumstances of his being, the unity of man, as man, is the same.

What that unity is it has been the object of the foregoing pages to illustrate and maintain.

It is admitted that the varieties due to the influences by which childhood is surrounded can hardly be de-

P

fined, such is the wide range of training—from simple
barbarism to wisest culture, but whatever the strange
extremes under which the human being is developed,
the essential attributes of humanity remain.

The savage may fatten the baby for a *bonne bouche ;*
the slave-holder may protect it and hold it as a bit of
useful property ; the infanticide may get rid of it as an
encumbering nuisance ; the priest may exorcise it as the
abode of devils, and cleanse it in the baptismal font ;
but if the conviction is, by the perusal of these pages,
fortified, that the child is what the Great Teacher
claimed for it—the child as such—the child essentially
—the object of the writer is attained.

The child as such is capable of possessing and
expressing the Spirit of Christ. Of all human beings
on this earth a *child* is most closely allied to the Christ
in the most essential attributes of the nature of Christ
—*Trust, Hope and Love.*

How soon, alas, in the little child are distrust,
doubt, and suspicion engendered by the injudicious,
often wicked conduct of those who have control over it!

How early are its springs of happy hopefulness
polluted, and sometimes dried up, by the hopeless
wretches who grudge the little ones the innocent pros-
pects of joy and mirth inviting them to larger life.

And how the unfolding affection of childhood to
sweet and kindly parental love, and even to all
sympathetic tenderness, is frozen by the cold blast of
hatred or indifference of self-enclosed hearts.

The age in which we live has given us a theology of childhood which presents a gratifying contrast to the theology of the dark ages.

The Christian ideal, through the Hymnology of our modern Sunday Schools, is happily realized, not only in its better sentiment and truer poetry, but even more remarkably by the exclusion of hymns which make children little devils, only fit for a world of devils.

The clouds of demoniacal darkness which had obscured, and sometimes obliterated the Eternal Father from the horizon of childhood, have largely been swept away, and a little child can now behold the divine glory in the face of Jesus Christ.

So far from overdrawing the picture of the loving Son of God the attempt has been quite inadequate. But let it be realized in a small degree that Jesus is what He proclaimed Himself to be, and the greatest stimulus will be given to parents and all who have the management of children, to value *them* as they have never done before.

We see our Lord in the hungry and thirsty, in the sick and in prison—let us not fail to see Him in the little child.

The great question discussed in these pages is most practical. As is the conception formed of the nature of the child so will be the method adopted in its religious education.

If childhood be explained by the doctrine on which John Wesley's dictum is founded :—

P 2

"As a rule children ought never to play,"

or on Augustus Toplady's definition :—

"Bubbling fountains of iniquity,"

the education of the child would logically necessitate a
very different method from that which we now pursue,
under guidance such as that of Henry Ward Beecher,
who says :—

"In dealing with children have *confidence* in them.—
Do not try to corner a child into *a lie.*—I have been
cornered into a good many lies.—*I knew I was right,*
and I was whipped until *I confessed I was wrong.*

If a child has done something that is wrong, as far
as possible avoid bringing an issue by which the fear of
the frown or the whip shall make him dodge into *de-
ception,* and try to *hide. That* is characteristic of the
animal nature—that is what the fox and hare do, and
that is what the *child* does under *such circumstances.*

Take care of your tenderness. The child may be
driven into a sin by you ; whereas by kindness and
gentleness you can lift him over the hard spot, and
set him down intact on the other side."

The following wise words from P. T. Forsyth are to
the point :—

"We have more faith than we used to have in
education. The natural man *may be* Christianised by
a conversion of some violence ; but the natural child,
if you would only *begin in time,* and respect its *natural-
ness,* is Christianised by education.

" Except ye be converted and become as little children &c."—The man is converted to the child, but the
child is *educated* to the ' man in Christ Jesus.' "

That the divine-human view of childhood is the
true one, is strikingly corroborated in the remarkable
practical unanimity with which men of all shades of
opinion express themselves, outside their ecclesiastical
and theological definitions and limitations. Cardinal
Manning writes : " The holiness of children is the very
type of saintliness ; and the most perfect conversion
is but a hard and distant return to the holiness of a
child."*

If the Venerable Bishop who wrote the following put
his thought about children into practice, one might
put the training of his offspring into the Bishop's care
with considerable satisfaction, regardless of his theological commitments : " No man can tell but he who
loves his children, how many delicious accents make a
man's heart dance in the pretty conversations of these
dear pledges ; their childishness, their stammering,
their little angers, their innocence, their imperfections,
their necessities are so many little emanations of joy
and comfort to him that delights in their persons and
society."

If the child is much indebted to those who discharge
their responsibilities to it, there is a very large account *per contra*, due to the child. This is briefly and
well put by the Rev. Thomas Binney :

* *Towards Evening.* Kegan Paul & Co., 1889.

" Every infant comes into this world like a delegated prophet, the harbinger and herald of good tidings, whose office it is to draw 'the disobedient to the wisdom of the just.' Infants recall us from much that engenders and encourages selfishness, that freezes the affections, roughens the manners, and indurates the heart; they brighten the house, deepen love, invigorate exertion, infuse courage, and vivify and sustain the charities of life."

Among the practical considerations arising out of this subject, especially in the present day of forced marches, of cramming, of prodigies, of spectacled boys and girls, and spinal affections, are the over-working and over-developing whips of tutors and examinations.

The Hon. Miss Murray in her Notes on Education, writes: "It once happened that an anxious mother asked Mrs. Barbauld at what age she should begin to teach her child to read? 'I should much prefer that a child should not be able to read before five years of age,' was the reply.—'Why then have you written books for children of three?' 'Because, if young mammas will be over-busy, they had better teach in a good way than a bad one.'—I have known clever precocious children at three years dunces at twelve,—and dunces at six particularly clever at sixteen!—One of the most popular authoresses of the present day could not read when she was seven. Her mother was rather uncomfortable about it, but said, that as *everybody did* learn to read with opportunity, she supposed that her child would do so *at last.* By *eighteen* this apparently slow genius paid the heavy but inevitable debts of her father from the profits of her first work and before long had published thirty volumes."

What would L. E. Landon say to the forcing processes of modern education, who wrote years ago of the children ?

How much they suffer from our faults,—
    How much from our mistakes,—
How often, too, " misguided zeal "
    An infant's misery makes.
We *over-rule*, and *over-teach*,—
    We curb and we confine,—
And put the *heart to school too soon*
    To learn *our narrow line.*
No ; only taught by love to love,
    Seems Childhood's natural task ;—
Affection, gentleness and love,
    Are all its brief years ask.

It cannot be too intensely realized, or too urgently enforced, that a little infant will never be, except when abnormally excited, more delicately sensitive than in its early stages of life. It is true of the organs of special sense. It is true of the brain, and of the formation of ideas. It is not less true of the emotions. And, above all, it is true of its spiritual faculty. Tom Hood recalls the fact, in his really delicate little poem, " I remember, I remember," which ends with the pathetic lines :

" It was a childish ignorance,
    But now 'tis little joy
  To know I'm farther off from heav'n
    Than when I was a boy."

We may be thankful that the evolution proceeds at a diminishing and not an increasing ratio, for only thus it is that earliest impressions are not only profoundest but most enduring.

"For the child," Richter remarks, "the most important era in life is that of childhood, when he begins to colour and mould himself by companionship with others. Every new educator effects less than his predecessor, until at last we regard all life as an educational institution. A circumnavigator of the world is less influenced by all the nations he has seen than by his nurse."

In the progress of the infant's development, the lower part of its being takes precedence of the higher. Its physical wants claim immediate attention. The child readily yields to the more imperative objective stimuli : as light to the eye, air to the lungs, food to the stomach, &c. But though its higher faculties are not so quickly developed, the most permanent effects are produced on the soul; and the strongest formative forces are those which touch its sentiments and awaken its affections. For the child, not less than the man, "does not live by bread alone." And as it advances in healthy development, what happens? The lower nature at length becomes subordinate to the higher, and the body comes to be regarded and treated as the humble servant of the soul.

But now, gentle reader, while we are contemplating the little child, we may ask where is God most truly seen ?

You say He is seen as He rides upon the storm ;— as He flies on the wings of the wind. I say He is perceived in the still, small voice. Do you see Him in the midnight glory of the starry heavens ? I see Him more in the tender twinkle of a little child's eye. Do you trace His voice in the majestic roll of the thunder, as it reverberates from cloud to cloud ? I hear His utterance, not distant but as a whisper in my ear, in the loving tones of a tender mother. Does the manifestation of His mighty mind impress you in the scathing flash of lightning ? I think it is infinitely nearer to me in the flash of wit which sometimes may be seen darting out of the clouds of ignorance of the humble peasant. The lightning may shatter the nerves. The earthquake may shake the clay taber- nacle. But God is not in the earthquake, He is not in the thunder, to the highest part of our being He never can be. The soul has no eye for physical light- ning,—no sense for earthquakes,—no ear for thunder, but is most susceptible to appeals to conscience,—to its affections—to its mind.

The subject which it was proposed to discuss, it is hoped has not been unfairly treated, in view of many accepted theories of human nature and misconceptions of the Wise Creator of our species, and the Holy Redeemer of our race.

The education of a child has not been the immediate purpose of the writer. Principles have been suggested, which must be based upon a true conception of the child's nature ; and it cannot be denied that a just apprehension of the nature of a child must lie at the foundation of any true theory and any wise and judicious practice of education.

INDEX.

*Just published, Fourth Edition, pp. 121, Imperial 8vo, Cloth,
Price 2s. 6d. nett.*

SONGS FOR LITTLE SINGERS

IN THE SUNDAY SCHOOL AND HOME

COMPOSED BY

HENRY KING LEWIS.

NOTICES OF PREVIOUS EDITIONS.

" Here are words and melodies admirably suited for the children in our homes and schools. Just the sort to make them sing with delight rather than as a task. Parents could not do better than purchase this volume."—*Word and Work.*

" Expresses the real feelings of childhood. The melodies are simple and pretty and such as children enjoy."—*Church Times.*

" We can heartily recommend this pretty book as supplying a want that has long been felt in giving the children songs to sing which they can understand and enjoy, and which express the real feelings of childhood."—*Practical Teacher.*

" The author has evidently sympathetic acquaintance with childhood and its needs, and simplicity and melody, without silliness, have been attained."—*The Wesleyan Methodist Magazine.*

" A delightful selection of songs and accompaniment very suitable for children at home or school."—*The British Friend.*

" The songs are varied from grave to gay, from the time for worship to the time for laughter and fun. The melodies are simple without being silly, and the harmonies are all within the range of young players."—*The New Age.*

" The words and music are alike within the comprehension of little ones, and are bright and joyous in character."—*Christian Leader.*

" It has evidently won its way to success by its merit. The composer has beautifully executed an idea of his own. Many of the melodies and accompaniments are really beautiful." —*Christian Commonwealth.*

" Its popularity is deserved, for the songs are all good, and the music is good also. This book is beautifully printed and bound. One of the cheapest and best things we have seen for a long time."—*Family Churchman.*

" A book with charming rhymes and sweet music. We have read and we have listened with pleasure. It will prove a favourite in the home."—*Baptist Messenger.*

" An excellent collection of songs and hymns for young folks. The words of the songs breathe happiness, beauty and love, and the melodies are usually admirably suited to the words."—*The Friend.*

" Mr. Lewis has studied the requirements of the children, and has fully met them in this delightful volume. Will be welcome wherever it goes."—*Methodist Sunday School Record.*

" We gladly recommend this charming book, which though originally intended for use in infant classes at school, is a welcome addition to the pleasures and instruction of home."—*Early Days.*

" We do not know of any collection of children's songs better adapted to its purpose than this one. It combines all the qualifications necessary to render it attractive to young learners—exquisite melody, simple yet effective harmony, and a perfect agreement between the words and the music."—*Educational Times.*

"Admirably arranged, and excellent in moral and spiritual tone. We have never seen a work of the kind we like better.........It should be circulated by thousands......... Parents, you should by all means purchase this."—*Evangelical Magazine.*

"A book of song thoroughly adapted to the little singers for whom it is intended. It consists of hymns and cheerful songs, not any of them above the capacity of intelligent children, set to airs which will be easily caught and remembered. We commend it to mothers, and to all who have the care and training of the young."—*Congregational Magazine.*

"Joyous songs are not only the delight but the requirement of childhood. Quick to recognise this, Mr. Henry King Lewis made a selection of the brightest and best, added a few of his own composition and set the whole to music, the airs being in strict keeping with the simplicity of the words. What infant-class would grow weary of singing, say with pianoforte accompaniment, such melodies as 'Suppose the Little Cowslip,' and lessons learned in song make an abiding impression?"—*Sunday School Times.*

"This collection of songs is vastly superior to much that 'little singers' are condemned to learn and sing in the present day. In fact there is an originality about some of Mr. Lewis's compositions that is quite refreshing. Amongst others we may mention the 'Morning Hymn,' 'Among the Children,' 'Alice's Supper,' 'Bethlehem,' 'The Grasshopper,' and 'Thy Kingdom Come,' as being superior both in the words and in the music to the general stock pieces which appear in programmes of many of the children's Choral Festivals which are of such frequent recurrence.
"We recommend all who have to do with these gatherings to obtain Mr. Lewis's book of Songs. Most of the pieces are capable of being sung by Sunday-School children, and what makes them especially valuable is that the composer has not sacrificed the educational object which all such gatherings should have in view to the mere gratification of the senses."—*The Church Sunday School Magazine.*

"Brightness, melody, simplicity, and adaptation to the child-nature, are the chief charms of this collection."—*General Baptist Magazine.*

"Mr. Lewis is evidently just the right person to write songs for the little ones......... His idea is thoroughly worked out. Though nowhere soaring above the capacity of his audience, his songs will be thoroughly appreciated by the elder ones. In fact, viewed as abstract musical compositions, they possess great intrinsic value. They are bright, melodious songs, which will be a long continuing source of the greatest pleasure to young and old."—*The Schoolmaster.*

"Persons who expect to find in this capital work songs of the 'Here we suffer' kind, are not likely to meet with much of what they want, but parents and teachers who wish to obtain words and music thoroughly adapted to the capacities and proclivities of children, will find such here in abundance......Simple and lively, without a trace of vulgarity. The work is intended more especially for infant class use, but will suit older children: and before publication most, if not all, the songs have duly undergone the scrutiny of a committee of 200 juvenile musicians, have been performed by them in public, and have pleased young and old alike."—*The Quaver.*

"This is a charming book for the young folk, and will prove a delightful present for the approaching season. Mr. Lewis is a wise and practical enthusiast in the matter of children's worship-song. Both the songs and music of this volume have borne the practical test of use in a large gathering of children, and those who have been privileged to hear the young singers know how well these compositions have borne that most searching of all tests. Some of the songs and all the music, are from the pen of the editor, and reflect very great credit upon his skill and taste. It should be added that the printing and binding of the volume are both very attractive."—*Christian World.*

"We welcome any special effort in the direction of songs and music for infants, for too often the ordinary hymns of the schools are theirs also. Mr. Lewis recognizes the claims of the little ones to more special provision, and he does somewhat to meet them here by this collection, which contains some new hymns, and some old favourites, but all set to music by himself. We heartily thank him for what he has done."—*Sunday School Chronicle.*

LONDON:
SIMPKIN, MARSHALL, HAMILTON, KENT & Co., Ltd.

www.ingramcontent.com/pod-product-compliance
Lightning Source LLC
Chambersburg PA
CBHW020109030726
47498CB00006B/2020